Amelia leaned forward, looking upset.

"What is it, Amelia?" Grace asked.

"Two soldiers who never went home. Two families thought them dead. Imagine the pain their families must have felt." Tears filled Amelia's eyes.

"When I read their letters and diaries, it seems like yesterday." Grace leaned her chin on her palm. "It's like John and Tom live now, with me."

"I have an idea," said Amelia, her face brightening. "Maybe they have descendants living right here! We could go to the courthouse to check the records and find their descendants."

Hannah looked curious. "Why would we do that?"

"Then we could do the same in their hometowns, and find the descendants from their families. And when Christmas comes, we can invite them all to Covington for a grand celebration and give them all copies of their ancestors' letters and diaries!" Amelia's eyes sparkled.

"A Christmas celebration? What a lovely idea," Grace said.

Amelia leaned against the porch rail, her mind racing. She could see it all: a light layer of snow on the ground, luminaries along the driveways, Cove Road decorated with holiday lights. How beautiful it would be!

Turn the page to read praise for Joan Medlicott's
enchanting Covington novels . . .

TWO DAYS AFTER THE WEDDING

"Join the ladies and the rest of the colorful cast of characters in the latest of Medlicott's popular, homey tales."

—*Booklist*

A COVINGTON CHRISTMAS

"This cozy, gentle read is sure to please Medlicott's many readers."

—*Library Journal*

"A pure charmer, a rich Southern tale about love and loyalty."

—*BookPage*

"Another charming addition to this delightful series . . . a beautiful story that will warm your heart and nourish your soul."

—*Fresh Fiction*

THE SPIRIT OF COVINGTON

"A must-read for women of all ages." —*The Tampa Tribune*

"A genuinely inspiring tale. The reader can't help but be moved by the 'ladies' and their progress." —*Library Journal*

"A winner. . . . The three ladies inspire by forming a community in which they thrive and find new careers and loves, all with dignity and autonomy." —*Publishers Weekly*

A Blue and Gray Christmas is also available as an eBook

Also by Joan Medlicott

The Covington Series

The Spirit of Covington
At Home in Covington
A Covington Christmas
Two Days After the Wedding
An Unexpected Family
Promises of Change

Other Books

The Three Mrs. Parkers
Come Walk with Me

A
Blue and Gray
Christmas

JOAN
MEDLICOTT

Pocket Star Books

New York   London   Toronto   Sydney

Pocket Books
A Division of Simon & Schuster, Inc.
1230 Avenue of the Americas
New York, NY 10020

This book is a work of fiction. Names, characters, places, and incidents either are products of the author's imagination or are used fictitiously. Any resemblance to actual events or locales or persons, living or dead, is entirely coincidental.

First Pocket Star Books paperback edition November 2010

POCKET STAR BOOKS and colophon are registered trademarks of Simon & Schuster, Inc.

For information about special discounts for bulk purchases, please contact Simon & Schuster Special Sales at 1-866-506-1949 or business@simonandschuster.com.

The Simon & Schuster Speakers Bureau can bring authors to your live event. For more information or to book an event contact the Simon & Schuster Speakers Bureau at 1-866-248-3049 or visit our website at www.simonspeakers.com.

Interior designed by Akasha Archer
Cover design by Laywan Kwan
Cover illustration by Robert Hunt

Manufactured in the United States of America

10 9 8 7 6 5 4 3 2 1

ISBN 978-1-4767-8698-8
ISBN 978-1-4165-9743-8 (ebook)

For my children

ACKNOWLEDGMENTS

Special thanks to Andrea Zimmermann, research librarian at the Cyrenius H. Booth Library in Newtown, Connecticut, for allowing me to see Newtown through her eyes. It was a treat to chat with John Vouros, a gracious host, along with his wife Jane, of the Dana-Holcombe House.

Thanks to Daniel Cruson, former history teacher, Newtown's historian, and president of the Archaeological Society of Connecticut for his splendid book, *A Mosaic of Newtown History*, which provided me with invaluable information about the history of Newtown. My thanks to acclaimed artist Patricia Barkman, for inviting Amelia and Milo into her lovely gardens and art studio and showing them her work. I am sincerely and deeply appreciative to all of them for their generosity and time. They brought Newtown, Connecticut, alive for me.

And to Karen Pulver, who dresses as a Southern lady married to a northern soldier for Civil War reenactments, 2nd Battery Vermont Light Artillery, whose knowledge of those times and the books she referred me to greatly enhanced the veracity of the letters; thank you, thank you.

1

The Battered Box

THE FALL DAY HAD turned chilly; a brisk wind
blew from the west. In the ladies' farmhouse,
flames danced behind faux logs in the fireplace,
casting a golden glow across the pale yellow
walls of the living room. Grace Singleton and
her housemates, Hannah Parrish Maxwell and
Amelia Declose, had pulled chairs into a circle
around a low table. Upon it sat a battered tin box
the size of two large shoeboxes.

Earlier that day, Hannah's husband, Max, had
strode into the house, his overalls streaked with
dirt and grime from carrying the box, which was

discovered while a foundation was dug for one of his historic restorations.

"Lord only knows how long it's been buried," he'd said. "The fellow on the backhoe said it looked like an old fishing box he inherited from his grandfather, who had it from *his* father. We broke the lock and opened it. Just a bunch of letters and a couple of small books inside, but I thought you ladies might like to check them out."

Intrigued, Grace had taken the box to the kitchen, scraped away layers of red clay dirt, and scrubbed it as clean as she could get it. One side looked as if it had been struck by a hammer, but the box had survived intact with no apparent damage to its contents: several small leather-bound diaries and bundled letters addressed in faded ink to folks in South Carolina and Connecticut. Dark and dented, the box sat now on their coffee table.

"Open it, Grace. Open it." Amelia's blue eyes gleamed with excitement. "Maybe it's a buried treasure."

"Books and letters, treasure?" Hannah's eyebrows shot up. "We'll be lucky if they don't crumble when we touch them."

Rusty hinges creaked as Grace lifted the lid and eased it back. Inside lay six packets, one of which had been untied. The remainder were bound with twine, frayed and crumbling in places.

A thrill of excitement raced through her and she eased the untied bundle of letters out as gently as she would lift a newborn babe from its cradle. The top envelope opened easily and Grace extracted two sheets of paper, which she spread on the table beside the box.

"It's to a Marianne Mueller, Little River Bend Community, Walhalla, South Carolina." Surprised, Grace looked from Hannah to Amelia. "We know where Walhalla is. We've eaten at The Steak House there. It's near Lake Jocassee, remember?"

Amelia nodded. "Can you make out the writing?" Her fair skin was pink with excitement, and she could hardly sit still.

"I'll try." Grace squinted at the faded words, then read aloud:

Dear Cousin,

I write to you, this bein' the year 1864 and the war ain't ended yet. Bein' so much alone, at times my mind plays tricks on me, specially when it's quiet like it was after my last battle, no guns roarin' or men screamin'. Sometimes, layin' in bed, safe now and far from war, I think back to that time when I was layin' in that rock-hard ditch, thinkin' I'm gonna die. Weren't nothin' but gray fog, hard mean pain, and my leg twisted, hurtin' bad. Them Yanks come at us out of nowhere, the blue coats yellin' and shootin' a cannon right atop us. The noise like to bust my head open. Cannon blast mustta sent me flyin', mustta dumped me in that there ditch. All's I could do was keep breathin' and stay alive. 'Twas the worst I was ever scared.

Fellow layin' next me in that ditch was a-wearin' a blue uniform stained with blood, and he raised up his hand, fingers bloody and clawin' the air. His face all mussed with dirt and gunpowder and filthy from war. That there Yank's alive, I thought. Let the bastard die. Then I thought, he's jus' a man like me, scared and sufferin' in this stinkin' hell.

They mustta give us up for dead. Guess we fooled 'em, I thought, and the pain gripped me so bad I thought, this here's my last breath. But the pain eased, and I lay there pantin', tryin' to gather my wits and strength to help myself and maybe the Yankee layin' next to me.

I'd mended plenty of animals on the farm at home and the broken parts of men in the war, 'cause there was never 'nough medics to carry the wounded from the field to the hospital wagon, and I'd carried many a man and helped in their care. The Yank aside me was bleedin' bad. I tore my shirt and turned, even with the pain it brung me, and tied off the Yank's wounds to stop the bleedin' and bandaged the gash on his head, all the time wonderin' why I was tendin' the enemy.

I laid back, then, and worried how I was gonna splint my broke leg, 'cause there weren't no wood about. If I could splint my leg, I could crawl outta this here ditch. Aside me, the fellow groaned, and I figured he'd never make it out.

My rifle was next to me, and I laid it next to my leg and tied it straight, though I wondered why, since I was gonna die anyways. Then I thought, damn well better die with the Yank than dyin' alone.

Then the pain came over me real bad again, and my mind went away again. When I came to, I muttered somethin' about bein' lost and a-headin' east.

The Yank groaned like he was awake then, and told me they was lost, too, their maps gone, officers dead of dysentery. They was scared, he tells me, and didn't know what to do. Someone loaded their cannon and sent a shot flying. He went flying. That's all he remembered.

Then he turned hisself over best he could and said his name, John Foster, and I said mine, Tom Mueller, and somethin' passed between us—and to hell with the war, I knew I weren't gonna crawl outta that ditch and leave him to die alone.

❧ 5 ❧

Grace looked up. "I can't make out the rest. It's too water stained." As she carefully folded the brittle paper and slid it back into the envelope, the ladies sat deep in their own thoughts.

Then Hannah said softly, "Amazing. That letter's more than a hundred years old. The war began in 1861, if I remember correctly, and ended with Lee's surrender to Grant at Appomattox in April, 1865. Here we have two soldiers from opposing sides left to die in a ditch on a battlefield in 1864, and Frank Hays's backhoe dug up that rusty, old box in our field."

"You know your history," Grace said, turning to Hannah. "I'm impressed."

Amelia dabbed at her eyes with her handkerchief. "How terrible, to be injured and left to die like that." Then her face brightened. "But they didn't die; they wrote those letters and diaries. How did they survive? How did they get to Covington?"

"Hopefully the other letters are in better condition." Hannah cleared her throat. "I'm sure we'd all like to know more about this Tom Mueller and the Yankee he helped."

Amelia nodded and looked at Grace. "Go through the packets, please, and see if you can find one of John's letters."

2

John's Letter

SITTING ON THE EDGES of their chairs, Hannah and Amelia watched as Grace gently lifted one packet after the other, examining the dates.

"This one, maybe," she said. "The writing on the envelope's different, a more refined hand, and it's dated 1864." The string broke even under Grace's gentle touch, and several envelopes fell from her lap to the floor.

Amelia picked them up and piled them neatly on the table beside the old box. "I hope it's a letter about the day he and Tom lay in the ditch."

Grace eased the first envelope open, carefully

unfolded the letter to skim it, then returned it to its envelope. Five letters later, a smile spread across her face. "I think this is the one we're hoping for. It's addressed to Dear and no name." Carefully smoothing the pages, she began to read:

My first thought, when consciousness returned and as pain overwhelmed me, was that I was going to die slowly and alone in some ditch on a mist-shrouded field far from home, surrounded by the corpses of men, horses, and the remains of shattered guns. The prospect filled my heart with anguish and it terrified me.

It wasn't easy, and only the good Lord knows how I managed to raise my head above the ditch; the pain that tore through me was the devil himself. A damp, low-lying mist hung over what had probably been a green cow pasture, now rubbed raw, destroyed by the pounding and scuffling feet of thousands of lost Rebs and Yanks struggling and dying over a piece of earth far from their homes.

My mind fastened on the skirmish—the rumbling supply wagons pulled by oxen, the stink of gunpowder, the roar of a cannon fired at Lord knows what, for no buildings stood in the field, no signal stations . . . and all about me were men dying where they'd fallen, screaming, moaning, blood gushing from their wounds.

My strength was ebbing from loss of blood, and I wondered how bad the soldier beside me was wounded. Would he try to kill me? If he did, I couldn't defend myself.

As I lay there waiting to die, I asked myself, why had I been so foolish, so idealistic, as to rush off to a war to keep the Union together? When I joined up we were called the Army of the Potomac, and for nearly a year we saw nothing of war, and passed the time sitting about camp, talking and playing cards, and I learned to smoke my first pipe, eat food with weevils, and fight lice.

My mind went back to another time my regiment was lost, closer to home, to Connecticut, early on in the war. We had reached our assigned location in the woods somewhere, and the supply wagon train never found us. The roar of battle sounded from over some hill, and we couldn't tell if it was near or far, or who would win, or if we would escape the woods alive. For many days we foraged to eat, ravenous soldiers huddled around a pit fire cooking potatoes we'd scavenged from some poor old woman's stash. War makes savages of good men.

It was then that Tom looked over at me and our eyes met and held, and something passed between us. We were not just soldiers and adversaries, but wounded men hoping to hang onto what life we had and find ease from pain. I wondered if he had brothers or sisters, if he was married, if his family kept slaves, if he had fought to keep them, or if he fought so that the South could leave the Union. We were fools, both of us, and I swore then that if we survived this pain and horror, I would respect his beliefs, whatever they might be.

Tom saved me. He kept me from bleeding to death. He helped me climb from the ditch. With his broken, splinted leg, he supported me as I struggled to reach Miss Ella Mae's wagon. She carried us away into the hills, tended us, and healed us. Ma believed in angels, and so do I. That day Tom and Miss Ella Mae Evans were my angels.

You could hear a pin drop as Grace finished reading John's letter.

Finally, Amelia broke the silence. "We must read all the letters. We must know more about Miss Ella Mae, what was she doing there, and how she saved their lives."

Grace's mind lingered on that brutal field of war, and she shivered slightly as she pulled herself back into the present century. "I'm curious to know who this woman was, too. We'll open them all and read them."

"I hope they're legible," Hannah said.

"So do I." Grace returned the letter to the box. "The two men write so differently. Tom's less educated—his writing's simpler, more terse, while John's flows out."

Hannah nodded. "I prefer Tom's account. He's clearly more rugged, a farm boy. And he's a good, kind fellow, or he'd have had no empathy for a Union soldier."

Amelia rubbed her arms. "Their letters give me gooseflesh. It must have been so terrible."

"War is always terrible." Hannah brought a hand to her heart. "Tom's writing may not be fancy, but it's real. Grace, find another of his letters or read from one of his diaries. I'd like to hear from him again."

Grace lifted out a small, leather-bound book and offered it to Hannah. "Would you like to read from Tom's diary?"

Hannah shook her head and waved her hands. "No, no. You do it. I prefer not to handle them."

"Why?" Grace asked. "We could take turns reading."

Hannah shrugged. "Though I'm the least religious of us, I find it somehow . . . sacrilegious to speak the words of these two men. But I'm eager to hear every word you read," she hastened to add.

Grace studied the women. She knew them well: Amelia,

sensitive and romantic; Hannah, skeptical and pragmatic. There were times when Hannah found Amelia's dreamy, almost childlike enthusiasm irritating, and times when Amelia found Hannah unfeeling. Yet with all their differences they had shared this home in Covington for the last eight years, most of the time harmoniously.

Before coming to Covington, they had met almost nine years ago at a dreary, boarding house in Pennsylvania, widowed, lonely, feeling rejected by family and the world. Pooling their financial and emotional resources, and against the wishes of their children, they had packed their belongings and moved here to an old farmhouse Amelia had inherited.

Their lives had metamorphosed then, opening like flowers in springtime. Hannah had recently married Max and they were deeply involved in historical preservation, re-creating the original Covington Homestead at Bella's Park, the land Max and Hannah owned at the end of Cove Road. Amelia had discovered a talent for photography and had published several coffee-table books that were sold in local stores. Grace had met her dear friend and companion Bob Richardson, and her volunteer work at Caster Elementary School sometimes consumed her—just as these diaries and letters were certain to consume her.

Back in high school she'd mainly been taught about the Civil War's battles and generals; the common soldier had hardly been mentioned. And now these diaries and letters had been unearthed.

Hannah coughed, drawing Grace back to Tom's dairy in her lap. "You going to read it?"

Grace opened the book to a random page. The date at the top was 1864, and alongside it was the word Battlefield.

A horse started up snortin' and wagon wheels was a-squeakin' then stoppin'. All's I could think was, they done come back to finish us off. Someone was turnin' things over, liftin' things, and gruntin' from the effort. It hurt, Lord, but it hurt, but I done raised up my head to see over that ditch.

A gray-haired old woman was pokin' about with a stick and starin' down at us. I couldn't tell if she was scared or mad we was alive, and she raised up her stick, lowered it, and bent closer. I seen her eyes, then, sad eyes sunk in a face wrinkled by age and weather.

She says she's just done buryin' her boy, her grandson, and come on us bleedin' and still livin', and she spat tobacco she'd been chewin'.

My throat was achin' but I done managed to tell her yes and that my friend here's hurt bad and my leg's broke. I was thinkin', Lord, I mustta got my head kicked by a mule, callin' this Yank a friend.

The woman was bent from work and age, and she pointed a finger outta a hand curled with the rheumatism, first at me, then John.

"You're one of us, and he's a Yankee," she says. Her laugh was more a cackle than a laugh, but it weren't mean like, just curious. Then she wanted to know who mended me.

I told her I done it, that I'd learned from the medics. Lord, how I prayed she weren't gonna walk off and leave us. If she had, we'd a been goners.

"Left you to die, the bastards." She straightened best she could, and her eyes narrowed like she was thinkin'. "I got me some strong corn liquor in the wagon. Couple of swigs'll help to kill the pain. If you can crawl outta that there ditch, I'll try my mightiest to get you outta here."

A laugh rose up in my chest at the thought of us drunk and staggerin' outta the ditch like we'd come from a tavern. I quick pushed that laugh back. This old woman was all the chance we had, and we'd best take it.

We drunk, then, and somehow drug ourselves to that wagon and hauled ourselves into it. She said her name was Ella Mae Evans. She done saved us, the good Lord bless her.

Next I remember was layin' on straw and wagon wheels clatterin' and we was goin' up a long hill. John done slept, and woke, and moaned plenty. I tried keepin' my eyes open to see where we was at, but all I seen was trees a-passin' over us. Next thing, the wagon stopped, and the old woman was urgin' me down from her wagon.

I opened my eyes and looked up at a sky as blue as the skies at home. It weren't easy, but we crawled off that wagon. Miss Ella Mae helped pull us up the slopin' steps to the porch of a old log cabin, with a saggin' roof and a low bench and firewood stacked alongside one end of the porch wall.

My bed was a corn-husk mattress in one corner of the room. After bein' in that ditch, it done seem like heaven itself. Days come and gone, and Miss Ella Mae give us medicine and lay salve on our wounds. When my pain eased, I seen gourds, like Ma hung for salt and flour and such things, on a wall near the fireplace, and above the fireplace in a wood rack I seen an old rifle.

At the other end of the room, Miss Ella Mae's bed was narrow, wood framed, with a thin mattress layin' atop the ropes. A rocker sat close by and a basket of cloth scraps, like Ma kept for quiltmakin' afore she passed. Then I seen the faded quilt folded neat on the end of the bed, and I felt a comfort inside me, and I knew Ma was a-watchin' over me. I blessed the old woman for savin' my life.

When I turned toward the wall near my bed, I seen chinkin' done fall out between the logs, and I seen the sky clear as I seen my hand. I knowed we was near a creek for the sound of rushin' water, and Lord above, the smell of cornpone and cracklins in that cabin set my belly beggin' for food.

"Some of the words are faded and I can't make them out." Grace turned the page. "Ah, this is better."

What potions Miss Ella Mae used to heal us, I'll never know, bein' as she was closed-mouthed 'bout her doctorin'. Kept us alive, she did. She carried us up to her cabin way far in these North Carolina Mountains where we was safe from bounty hunters. She treated us like we was kin and done nursed us to health, Lord bless her soul.

❧❧

Hannah glanced at her wristwatch and interrupted, "I'm going to have to leave soon. Max is waiting for me. I'd rather stay, but we're trying to locate the curing house of the Covington Homestead. We're not sure how close it was to the main cabin."

She and Max had undertaken a major project, re-creating the original homestead of the Covington brothers, who had settled the area in the late nineteenth century. It required patience, which Hannah was short of, and research, which was mainly done by her daughter Laura.

"Stay a while longer, please. With everyone so busy lately, we spend less time together." Grace longed for the camaraderie of their early years in Covington, when the three of them came together in the afternoons on their porch to share the day's events over a cup of tea. Reading these diaries and letters of two Civil War soldiers could draw them back to the way it had been.

"The war part is so sad, but it's gratifying that Tom helped John and that Ella Mae Evans helped those men." Amelia clasped her hands in her lap. "Out of so much pain and horror, goodness comes."

"Two men, sole survivors of a horrible battle," Hannah said. "Makes sense they'd help each other."

"Not necessarily. Tom could have turned away and let

John bleed to death. He chose not to." Amelia's voice rose. "And Ella Mae Evans must have been devastated at the loss of her grandson. She could have walked away."

Grace recognized an argument brewing. "Could, would, should—the fact is, Tom's kindness and Ella Mae Evans's generosity of spirit tell a lot about their characters, who they were."

Hannah rose to leave. "I do have to go, but I'm eager to hear about their lives. Don't read without me, please?"

"We wouldn't do that," Grace replied.

Hannah opened the door, letting in a cool blast of air. Fall had burst upon the land early in October, and the hillsides were a patchwork of yellows, rusts, and peaches.

Grace reached for the light wool shawl she had set on a nearby chair and pulled it around her shoulders. Her finger traced the edge of the diary in her lap.

"I wonder about fate, about Miss Ella Mae finding her grandson dead, yet stopping to help two wounded soldiers. You're right, Amelia. In her grief, she could have simply walked away. I wonder how long they stayed with her."

"I wonder if they repaired that sagging roof of hers." Amelia said.

Grace held up the diary. "Well, there's a lot to be read. I'm sure we'll find out."

3

Life-Altering Choices

❧ ❧

DAYS PASSED, AND THE ladies hadn't found time to sit and read from the letters and diaries again. Unable to resist, Grace took several letters and a diary to bed with her and scanned them, trying to create a time-line for the men, sometimes unsuccessfully, sometimes successfully.

When next they met to read, Grace held up a letter. "I've tried to put these in order, and I've marked Tom's letters #1 and John's #2." She hesitated, concerned that Hannah or Amelia might resent her getting ahead of them, but they looked eager for more. "So, this is a letter of John's."

❧ ❧

We owe our lives to Miss Ella Mae. She's alone and sad from her losses. As the weeks pass, as we gain back our strength, we chop her wood. Tom knows about building, and I help him the best I can. We built a woodshed close by the porch, for hers had fallen down due to time and weather. It's late December and we filled the new shed with wood for the winter, which is coming on fast with freezing nights and blustery days. We carry water from the stream, close by and running full and clear.

I help Tom fell trees and split firewood into small pieces, so that it appears that Miss Ella Mae cut them herself. We pile them onto her wagon and she carries them into the village, which is a ways from us, and sells the wood for money or exchanges it for a goat or a chicken or other goods for cooking. She goes alone, for we must stay hidden so no one will ask why we aren't fighting or tell bounty hunters our whereabouts.

As the days and weeks pass into months, Tom and I grow closer. He's becoming like a brother to me, closer than my own brother at home. We talk, sometimes, about maybe not going home after the war, about staying here with Miss Ella Mae. She has no kin to do for her, and we owe her our lives. If we stay, we'll build a room onto the cabin, for it's small with the two of us huddled close on our corn-husk mattress, and Miss Ella Mae having no privacy, until Tom built a wood frame screen. We cut pine branches and covered the frame and stood it in front of her bed. I admire how handy Tom is with a hammer, saw, and nails. He's promised to teach me.

My arm is still weak from my wound; the cut was deep and healed slowly, as did the deep gash on my leg. I do better hauling branches than cutting them off trees, better stacking wood than chopping it. Tom says he doesn't mind doing the harder work. My time will come in the spring, he says, when we hitch the horse and plow the field. Spring is months away. Please the Lord, I'll be stronger then. If the war is raging, we will be here, but if it ends, will I stay or begin the long trek home?

I know nothing of farming, of country life, and I miss my hometown of Newtown in Connecticut, my uncle's mill where I worked in the office keeping books, my cousin's button factory, and the general store where I sold goods and kept books.

I miss my ma and pa, even Emily and our little

Iris. Staying here means I will never see them again. The war will end some day, and if I don't go home, in time they'll think me dead and Emily will marry again. Why does this thought not make me sad?

Ours was too young a marriage, after a night in the barn, making love in the hay with no thought to a baby. We weren't suited to each other. She wanted a house, nice things to fill the house, and more babies. I wanted to travel, to wander. Was that behind my determination to fight for the Union, the spur to my patriotism? Was going to war my way to leave Emily, Iris, and responsibility behind? Shame, I tell myself, shame on me for behaving thus. But I don't feel shame. It was a union that should not have been, save for her father's shotgun and my father's pride.

I lie awake at night and puzzle over what to do. We are, in a sense, deserters, for we healed and never returned to war. I would like to tell Ma that I'm alive and well, but if I send letters home, word might reach those who would hunt for us and haul us back to the battlefield. That, I could not bear.

Tears filled Amelia's eyes. "But even if he and his wife weren't well suited, how could be leave his little daughter?"

Hannah shook her head. "Didn't you hear what he wrote? Emily got pregnant, and that's why they got married. Sometimes we have to make hard choices. John had a chance at a new life in Covington. You're overly romantic, Amelia. Not everything has a happy ending."

Amelia pouted. "After all they'd been through, I want them to be happy and live good lives, wherever they stayed."

"Let me finish his letter," Grace said.

Last night, Miss Ella Mae cooked venison stew that filled our bellies and warmed our souls. The night was warmer than usual, and for a time Tom and I sat on the old bench on the porch. We sat quiet awhile, until Tom said he'd made up his mind to stay with Miss Ella Mae. His ma's dead and his pa married a wife he didn't much like, and there were plenty at home to help, sisters and brothers too young to go to war. He hadn't left a wife or girl behind.

Then Tom said Miss Ella Mae had told him that when the war's done, if we're still here, she's gonna tell everyone we're family—nephews or cousins who found her after the war. He's thinking to take her name,

Evans, and said, "I'll stay with Miss Ella Mae till she
passes on."

Then Tom asked what I was thinking, and I told
him about Emily and Iris.

He said he envied me having someone to go home
to, and my stomach squeezed hard at his words, as I,
too, was thinking to stay with Miss Ella Mae.

Grace rubbed her chin. "That's the end of this letter. So many forgotten people."

Amelia looked confused. "What do you mean, Grace?"

"The women and children left to fend for themselves in these mountains. What were the men thinking when they trotted off to war? They didn't have slaves or plantations here. I bet they took the best horses, too. What a struggle it must have been for the women and children just to survive! No wonder Tom decided to stay and take care of Miss Ella Mae. She cared for him like a mother."

"I wonder what John decided to do," Amelia said softly.

"Enough for today," Hannah declared, standing. "That's in the past, and we all have things to do today and tomorrow."

4

Night Thoughts

LATER THAT EVENING, LYING in bed, Grace found it impossible to wipe the Civil War soldiers from her mind. She detested war. Was war endemic to human nature? It seemed to her that men who made war barely allowed sufficient time for the next generation to grow up before sending a new crop of young men off to die in a war: Korea in the fifties, Vietnam in the seventies, and now Iraq. And for what: land, power, control, and wealth? If women ruled the world, would they dispatch their sons to battle so willingly? She didn't think so.

Grace turned on the bedside lamp. There was

no point in trying to sleep, with her mind all a jumble. What had John and Tom intended to do with those neatly bundled letters and all their diaries? Had they buried them up there on that hillside? Probably.

But why? Had some urgent, unexpected need forced them to vacate the land? Had there been a local issue over land or water rights? Had there been a fire and the box lost in the rubble? Had they simply lost interest over time, set the box aside and forgotten about it? She would never know.

Grace straightened her sheet and pulled the soft blanket up across her chest. She loved this time of year; loved the crisp, cool nights, and kept her windows open to hear the creek by the house. Had the men stopped by this very creek for water, or to wash up at the end of a long, hot day? Maybe in time, the letters and diaries would answer her many questions.

SITTING ON THEIR FRONT porch the following day with Hannah and Amelia, Grace opened one of Tom's letters and began.

I never thought to walk again, but five months is gone, and I'm a-standin' on both feet and walkin' like a man. I worries for John, 'cause he wakes at night screamin' from fearful dreams. He ain't wont to tell 'em to nobody. He's seen more of fightin' than me and it's stayed in his head. None of Miss Ella Mae's remedies ain't gonna fix that.

Can't tell about John, what he's gonna do or say. We is sure different, but I loves him like he was my brother. One evenin' we was sittin' out on the front porch on that old wood bench, me and John and Miss Ella Mae, and she told us how her husband brung her here as a bride long years past. She set beside him in that wagon, joltin' along over rutted roads, and inside the wagon was all their worldly goods: the rocker alongside her bed, pots, pans, tools for buildin' and plantin', and what few clothes they had, and a lot of hope in their hearts. They was young, she said, and happy. She raised a son here. Why God ain't blessed 'em with more children she don't know, for she done prayed long and hard over it.

When her husband, Wayne, (her son was named Wayne, too, and they called him Junior) passed on, she stayed in the cabin he'd built her and tried ekin' out a livin' from the land and a few chickens and goats.

The Lord giveth and the Lord taketh away, she said, and she told us 'bout her son Junior's wife, and how she done passed on givin' them their grandson, the boy she'd lost on the field where she found us scoundrels. She grinned when she said that. I dunno why Miss Ella Mae liked to call us scoundrels, but she always done it with a laugh or a grin.

She told us many things, 'bout how one year they'd had plenty rain, and the rivers run full and fast, and plenty cabins was taken by risin' water. Junior gone on down to help a family that lost everything, and the water done swept him off. Never did find his body to give him a proper burial. She raised his boy, Joseph, the one got hisself killed down on that field.

I felt real sad for Miss Ella Mae. The Lord sent her to be the mother taken from me by sickness when I was a boy. When I told her I was stayin' with her, she pressed my hands hard and tears come to her eyes. To my eyes, too. That's when John said he was stayin', too. I opened my mouth to ask 'bout his wife and child, but he made me a sign to hush my mouth and I did.

Later, John told me he weren't right in his head no more, what with the dreams. He can't shake the things he's seen and done from his mind. He wouldn't say what them things were. Just that he wouldn't be good no more for his wife or child, so let 'em start new lives without him.

I thought, if I loved a woman hard, nothin' would stop me from goin' home to her, and I wondered about their life, but that weren't no time to ask.

Later he told me, "I'll do like you and take Miss Ella Mae's name. John Evans sounds pretty good, I think." We shook hands, knowin' we was startin' new lives.

Amelia leaned forward, looking upset.

"What is it, Amelia?" Grace asked.

"Two soldiers who never went home. Two families who thought them dead and lost to them forever. Imagine the pain their families must have felt, when they could have rejoiced if they'd known they were alive." Tears filled her eyes.

No one spoke for a time. Finally, Grace said, "It sounds as if Tom didn't have strong ties back home. Blood isn't always thicker than water."

"Ladies, let's try not to second guess. People have reasons why they do things and it happened a long time ago," Hannah said.

"When I read their letters and diaries, it seems like yesterday." Grace leaned her chin on her palm. "It's as if John and Tom's hopes, fears, and dreams transcend time and space. It's like they live, now, with me."

Amelia rubbed her arms. "It's like that for me, too. What if you'd been Tom's father or John's mother or wife? I can't bear to think of how they must have suffered."

"Then don't think about it," Hannah said impatiently.

Amelia ignored Hannah, her face brightening. "I have an idea. They both took the name Evans. If they stayed in this area, if they married, there'll be marriage, birth, and death records. Maybe they have descendants living right here! We could go to the courthouse to check the records and find their descendants."

Hannah looked curious. "Why would we do that?"

"Then we could do the same in their hometowns using their real names, and find the descendants from their families. And when Christmas comes, we can invite them all to Covington for a grand celebration and give them copies of their ancestors' letters and diaries!" Amelia's eyes sparkled.

"A Christmas celebration? What a lovely idea," Grace said.

Unimpressed, Hannah said, "That's really a long shot. It's already November. We'd never have time to hunt down all the people involved."

"We could try, Hannah. It would be fun, and it might be a blessing for the original families to know what happened to a relative who went off to war and never returned."

"People this many generations later don't even know about Tom or John, and probably wouldn't care," Hannah replied.

"But maybe they *would* care." Grace walked over to Hannah and took her hand in hers. "A lot of people are interested in genealogy these days. That's how Amelia inherited the original farmhouse in Covington. It gave us a place to come, to make a new life."

Hannah smiled at Grace. "Well, maybe it'll work. I'm going inside to pack up a few things; I'm sleeping over at Max's tonight. Let me know what you two decide and how you plan to do it." She went into the house, letting the door close behind her.

Amelia rose from her rocking chair and leaned against the porch rail, her back to Grace, her mind racing. She could see it all: a light layer of snow on the ground, luminaries along the driveways, Cove Road decorated with holiday lights; Max's big farmhouse across the road, Brenda Tate's and her daughter Molly's homes, the Cove Road Church, the Herrills and the Craines, and Bob's cottage, all trimmed out with lights. How beautiful it would be!

"Picture it, Grace: Christmas trees in every yard decorated with lights. We could have a welcoming ceremony, a beautiful Christmas Eve service at the church, and Christmas luncheon or dinner in the church hall." She paused for a moment. "I wonder what kind of Christmas they had with Miss Ella Mae back then. Did you find anything about that when you were sorting the letters, Grace?"

"I didn't, but it was probably quite plain and simple. I'll try to find it."

Amelia sank into her rocking chair. "I worry about John being so scarred by the war. I wonder if he ever felt right again?"

Grace tucked the letter into her apron pocket and sat next to the rocker Amelia had reclaimed. "Remember when Randy Banks returned from Iraq? He had terrifying dreams. Every little noise sounded like gunfire, and he reacted as if he were under attack. He was certain he'd never be his old self, and his depression worsened until he attempted suicide."

Amelia covered her mouth with her hand. "Of course I remember. That was awful, and he was lucky they got him to the veterans' hospital in time. He's much better now, isn't he?"

"Yes. He's started at AB Tech, training to become a paramedic. Randy will make it, but not without lots of help—especially from Bob." A pained look crossed Grace's face. "So many veterans are never free from the hell that lives in their memories. What a terrible price to pay."

Amelia slowed her rocker. "I wonder how long it took

for Tom and especially John to recover, to pick up their lives and go on? No one knew about post-traumatic stress then. How did they cope?" She sniffled, trying to hold back tears.

Grace handed her a tissue from her pocket. "Randy's counselor at the V.A. hospital told me that some veterans never fully recover." Grace remembered the sadness she had felt at the counselor's words and shook her head to banish the thoughts. "So, what do you think, Amelia? Shall we try to find Tom's and John's relatives?"

Amelia nodded. "Where should we begin? What should we do?"

"I'll try to find Miss Ella Mae's grave. I'll visit all the old graveyards in Madison County, and ask Randy to go with me. Hannah will help, I'm sure. I'll ask her to drop in at the newspaper office in Marshall and see how far back their records go."

"I'll check marriage records at the courthouse in Marshall," Amelia volunteered. Then she looked at Grace, and asked anxiously, "Are you staying over at Bob's tonight?"

Grace's longtime companion lived close by in a cottage on their land, and although his lights were clearly visible, Amelia was never comfortable alone in the farmhouse at night. She would look under her bed, behind the shower curtain, and in her closet; then she'd lie awake all night, watching, listening, and worrying.

"What if you were to see a pair of men's shoes in your closet?" Hannah had once asked her.

Amelia had shrunk back and stared at Hannah in utter disbelief before bursting into tears and running from the room.

"Why did you say that?" Grace had asked. Rarely did Hannah annoy or upset her, but that comment surely had.

"She's being childish. We had an alarm system installed especially for her, and lights on every corner of the exterior of this house. A rabbit runs by, and they go on. I have to draw my curtains at night not to be disturbed by those lights. Yet nothing's enough. Amelia ought to grow up."

"We all have our quirks and fears," Grace had replied. She had suggested to Amelia that she might benefit from a counselor, to help her get to the root of her fears, but although Amelia agreed, she never used the phone number Grace had offered her.

Now Grace replied, "No, I'm staying home. What say we stir up a batch of cookies and have a game of gin while we're waiting for them to bake?"

Amelia sighed with relief. "Oh, yes. I'd like that."

5

Cookies and Conversation

AMELIA AND GRACE HAD just reached the kitchen when they were joined by Hannah, a small overnight bag in her hand. "I'll be going shopping with Max. We're changing all the lightbulbs at his house, and we're going green in all the offices at Bella's Park. I'll buy them for this house, too."

"Can we afford to buy all those energy-efficient lightbulbs at one time?" Grace asked. "They're expensive. I was thinking to get them a few at a time." Her hand went to her throat. "There are times when I feel choked, like when I fill up my car at the gas station. I can't afford to go on paying over four dollars a gallon for gas, and they say it's going even higher. When I go to the market now, I don't buy anything that's not on the list. I'm stunned at the price of food. That's why I cook us so many chicken casseroles; they go a long way."

"Why haven't you said something about this, Grace? We could contribute more money to the food kitty each month," Hannah said.

Amelia turned to her, anger flaring. "And just where are Grace and I to get that money from, pray tell?"

Hannah looked startled, then a car horn blew from their driveway. "That's Max. I have to go. I'm sorry. I'll get the lightbulbs, and you can repay me whenever you can. And we'll talk about the food budget later, okay?" She waited a moment for their reply. Getting none, she said, "I'm off, then," and moments later they heard the front door close.

Grace sank into a chair at the kitchen table and motioned Amelia to do the same. "Listen to us, Amelia. We can't let money drive a wedge between Hannah and us."

"No, we can't," Amelia agreed. "Hannah's not around here as much as she used to be, and I guess she isn't as aware. I used to have spending money for whatever I needed or wanted. Now I have trouble making my money last until the end of the month. My books aren't selling as well because book buyers feel the crunch, too, and the price of my photography materials has sky-rocketed."

Grace nodded. "We shouldn't be mad at Hannah; we didn't tell her we're feeling pinched. I've been thinking, and I am going to ask Brenda if there's any part-time work at the school."

When the three women had first moved to Covington, they had set up a bank account into which they contributed funds each month for food and household expenses. With inflation, the price of everything—food, utilities, taxes, and insurance on the house and cars—had increased. But their incomes, except for Hannah's, who was married to Max now and a partner in the development of Bella's Park, had remained pretty much the same.

"There's always some change over which we have no control," Grace said. "With gas so expensive, I've cut way back on my driving. I used to go into Asheville just to pass the time some days. I don't anymore, and when I go, I take a long list of Must Do's." To calm herself, she got up and began collecting the ingredients for the cookies.

Amelia slid a cookie sheet from the cabinet. "Maybe that's why I think so much about Tom and John—it takes my mind off my money crisis. I think about them when I'm driving places, and at night when I'm in my room, I see Tom settled here with a wife and children, and I imagine the family sitting about a fire.

"Did they have caroling here in the mountains back then, do you think? Maybe Tom's family got all dressed up and went caroling." She smiled, pleased at the thought. "After all he'd been through, I want him to have a good life. And John, too, of course."

"I hope we're able to bring their families together," Grace said. "It would be like Christmas past and present. That would be wonderful, don't you think?"

She added sweetener to the butter she'd placed in a bowl, and handed Amelia a wooden spoon. "Mix this until the butter's soft, will you, please?"

Amelia mixed with vigor for a few minutes, then slowed. "Grace, what if one of the families isn't interested in meeting unknown relatives? Maybe they'll be angry that the men chose not to come home."

"Don't think negatively; just mix," Grace said. "I'm waiting to add the eggs and flour."

Amelia gave the butter a few more stirs. "If need be, I'll go to South Carolina and talk to Tom's family."

"That's a fine idea. Maybe Mike will go with you. Mix, please?"

"If he's around," Amelia said. "He takes people on photography workshops. This next one's in Central America." Her hand slowed again.

Grace sighed. "Give me the bowl." She finished blending the butter and sugar, and added the eggs and dry ingredients. "Butter that baking sheet, will you? Very lightly."

"Grace." Amelia smeared butter on half the cookie sheet. "What if one of the families doesn't want to celebrate with us?"

"You'll charm them. If anyone can charm people into changing their minds, you can."

Amelia finished buttering and shook her head. "I won't go up north; that's just too expensive. Walhalla is much closer."

"Do whatever feels right to you. Now, put these bowls in the dishwasher, and I'll drop the dough on the cookie sheet and stick it in the oven. Then we can have a game of gin."

As they played cards, Grace smiled, thinking how exciting it would be to embark on a quest to find the men's families and hopefully reunite them. What if Hannah was right and the relatives had no interest in meeting one another? So many generations had passed. Bob would say she was meddling again, this time in the lives of men long dead and buried. But she had to try, for John and Tom seemed so real to her.

The timer on the stove pinged, and Grace set the tray on a rack on the counter to cool. "I believe nothing happens by accident," she told Amelia. "The box came into our hands for a reason, and this may just be it. I'll look through the papers for the date of Miss Ella Mae's death. That's a good place to start."

Late that night, Grace skimmed letters and dairies seeking information about Miss Ella Mae's death. But before she found the information she sought, words of John's marriage popped out at her:

> It's but two days since I married Jenny Banks, Lord, but you know that. It's now several years since the war's ended, yet I don't feel guilty I didn't go home. That's a sin, I know, and I beg your forgiveness, Lord. You, more than anyone, know that Emily and I didn't get on well. Surely, with the war ending and men returning home, she's found a good husband. My heart would be

at ease if I knew that this was so, that she and Iris have a good home. But I have no way to know that, and that is a cross that I must bear, along with knowing the pain I have caused Ma and Pa.

I remind myself, Lord, that it was You who sent me to the pounding where I first saw my Jenny's lovely face. I didn't want to go, didn't even know what it was, but Tom and Miss Ella Mae pressed me.

"Mary and Frank Barnwell lost everything they owned when their home burned down," Tom said.

"And it's the custom." Miss Ella Mae was firm about that. "They might have got them a new house now, but they ain't got nothin' to put inside: no food, nothin' but a used bed and a chair given by the church choir. You got to go with us and bring a pound of something—sugar, cornmeal, beef, even a pot or a ladle."

So Tom and I went to town, which was no more than a general store, a barber shop, a blacksmith, a coffin maker, and a tavern, and we bought a pound of flour each. Then we dressed the best we could and accompanied Miss Ella Mae after church.

Many men had helped build the Barnwells' new cabin, and all the gifts were laid out on a long table in the front yard. I saw many pounds of butter and lard, meal, sugar, salt, and flour, a chick in a crate, a rib of pork fresh slaughtered. There were pots and pans, bedding and pillowcases, a child's cradle and small rocking chair, and more.

I saw Jenny there, a tall girl close to my own height, with flaxen hair and eyes blue as a summer sky, and Lord, my heart opened like a flower. I loved Jenny the moment I laid eyes on her, and she saw me and blushed and looked away, and I knew she felt it, too.

And now we are two days wed. Lord, I admit to you alone how scared I was when I stepped into the church. My sins are many and my heart was heavy. I have been to war and killed men. I have chosen not to return north to my home. I have abandoned wife and child. I felt unworthy to enter your holy house.

But Jenny took my hand and led me up the steps. "No matter what your sins," she said softly, "there's One who will always forgive you and take you to His bosom."

And so I stepped inside, and wept for the joy of it, and I silently told my many sins and begged Your forgiveness. As I sat on that hard wood bench, the church crude and primitive compared to my church in Newtown, my heart opened to receive Your love *and forgiveness. And it was then that the bad dreams finally eased.*

I have gone to Your house every Sunday since with my beloved Jenny. Had I loved Emily this way I would have crawled to Connecticut when the war ended, but it is better so. With Your love and grace, Emily will find her own true love as I have found mine.

Our wedding was a joyous event. Everyone in the town thinks that Tom and I are long-lost kin to Miss Ella Mae. Many speak of our resemblances to a cousin or to Uncle Ed, Miss Ella Mae's long deceased brother. They believed our story, that we found each other and met across the trenches at night. For it's true that cousins and brothers fought on opposite sides of the war, and at night, when the fighting stopped, they met to speak of family and friends at home. So now Miss Ella Mae's neighbors and the townfolks shake our hands and say how lucky she is that we found her, for they feared for her living alone so far from town.

Tom stood up for me at my wedding, but when we woke that joyful day, we found Miss Ella Mae ailing. I would not marry without her at the church, so we fixed the small wagon (we have two wagons now) comfortable for her with quilts and pillows, which we have plenty of now, as I work in a bigger town close by called Mars Hill one day a week, keeping books for Mr. Aubrey Pims at his general store. The rest of the days, I farm my land and raise cattle.

Though she protested, we lifted Miss Ella Mae off the wagon and carried her into the church and set a good chair next to a pew, where she sat like a queen, and indeed to Tom and me, she is one.

I stood alongside the minister and watched my lovely Jenny walk down the aisle accompanied by her father, a good man and a merchant from the town of Mars Hill. He was not happy Jenny was marrying a farmer, which is what I have become, and I'm proud to be one.

No daughter of his would marry without music, he said, so he donated a fine organ to the church. And I watched my Jenny walking down the aisle toward me in her fine white gown and "Amazing Grace" playing on that organ, it being the only song the organist had learned.

Miss Ella Mae gifted me a fine piece of land with pasture and a place for a vegetable garden, and Tom and our neighbors helped me build my bride a house. Not a log cabin, but a house with flat cut wood sides like at home, and a front porch with a railing in front

*and wide steps with railings on either side. From our
new porch, we can see the lights of Miss Ella Mae's
cabin. Tom lives with her still, though he's courting
a fine, buxom young widow named Glory and is
building a house of his own near Miss Ella Mae's with
a room for her, as he means for her to live with them
after he marries.*

Happy to read such news, Grace skimmed further in the
dairy. Many pages later, nearly to the end of the small book,
was a simple statement:

*This day, June 8ᵗʰ in this year 1872, dear Lord, I
beg that you take to your bosom our beloved Miss Ella
Mae Evans, passed from this earth on Sunday morning
last. This day we laid her to rest on the hilltop in the
cemetery beside her husband, Wayne, and her good
friend Maggie Benson. Tom and I wept mightily at
her passing. My Jenny, big with child, and me holding
our son, Tommy, and his Glory, also big with child,
and next to them her three little girls, stood close by to
comfort us in this time of our grief.*

Tears came to Grace's eyes. As she closed the diary she
squelched the urge to dash into Amelia's room to share this

news, but since it was three a.m., she would wait and read this part of the diary to them tomorrow.

Amelia's idea had taken firm hold in her mind. With or without Hannah, she and Amelia would begin at once to try to find the soldiers' descendants and invite them here this very Christmas.

6

Graveyard on the Hill

IT WAS THEIR FIFTH graveyard in as many days. Randy Banks and Grace had driven for over an hour through a valley, along a rushing river, and up a steep hillside to reach it. The rutted path leading up to the gravesites was demanding, especially for Grace in the chilly weather. Runnels chiseled by heavy rainfall hindered their progress, and they had to walk very carefully to avoid twisting an ankle.

"Take my arm," Randy said. "Let me help you over those roots."

"What were they, old apple trees?" Grace stepped over a gnarled root.

"That's right," Randy said. "Used to be an orchard, looks like. Ain't no one tended 'em in years."

At the crest of the hill, they wandered along the rows of gravesites, finding weed-obscured stone and wood markers, on many of which the words were illegible. Those that they could decipher were not useful: Lucian Farrelly: 1805–1856; Margaret Banks: Beloved Wife: 1801–1850; Sweet Baby Arlene McKinny: May 1812–June 1812.

Grace stood beside the toppled headstone of a James Greeley, who had lived to the ripe old age of ninety-five, and wiped her face with her handkerchief. "I don't think this is the right place."

Randy agreed, and they moved slowly and carefully down the hill, past upright, slanted, and fallen markers. Randy bent to read any legible names and dates. As he completed each row, he called to Grace, "Ain't nobody named Evans here."

Grace sighed. "This graveyard is a mess. Who are these people who don't visit their relatives? I want to find them and shake them."

"Mrs. Grace, you're raisin' up your blood pressure." The young man adored Grace. She had come into his family's life years earlier, when she had tutored his sister Lucy at Caster Elementary School. Grace had stepped into the void when his father died suddenly, and had helped his mother find a job, a new home closer to town, and helped his sisters and himself pick up and get on with their lives.

She had begged him not to enlist in the army, and had cried when he was assigned to Iraq. After his return, after being called to the house by Lucy to witness his bizarre behavior, she had urged him to seek help. When he'd tried to kill himself, Grace had dragged Bob to his bedside at the veterans' hospital, and Bob, a veteran of the Korean War, had become Randy's friend and mentor. This morning he had heard Bob argue with Grace about her search.

"It's just gonna raise your blood pressure. If graveyards are untended, there're probably no relatives around. People here take care of their cemeteries, and some families have yearly reunions near or in them," Bob had said, and silently Randy had agreed.

Now Grace wiped her red face. "I hate to admit it, but Bob was right." She sank onto a large rock. "I'm exhausted, Randy. The climb was so steep, and we didn't bring enough bottled water."

After she'd rested, Randy helped Grace to her feet and slipped his arm about her waist. "We'll walk slowly so as you don't slip."

"And the next time we'll bring snacks and more water," Grace said.

Randy hoped there wouldn't be a next time. As far as

he was concerned, they'd climbed enough hillsides and trudged through enough old cemeteries. They were creepy places and left him feeling uneasy.

AT BREAKFAST THE NEXT day, the ladies shared their findings.

Grace declared failure. "I found nothing, and I can't climb any more hills to old graveyards."

Amelia reported that at the county courthouse she had found a Thomas Evans married to a Melinda Jones on September 15, 1867, a Thomas Evans who married a Lucy Buckner in 1871, Thomas Evans and Jenny Lou Ebsen, who were married in 1869, and Thomas Evans and Mary Faine, who had married in September of 1872. "We'll have to check out the last three: Tom and Lucy, Tom and Mary, and Tom and Jenny Lou," Amelia said.

"Look for a Tom who married a woman named Glory," Grace said. "I found a John Foster Evans who married Jennifer Louise Banks."

Hannah looked satisfied as she reached across the table for the salt shaker and liberally salted her eggs. "I happened to be in Marshall the other day, so I stepped into the newspaper office. They have old obituaries on microfilm." Hannah sipped her coffee, then set her cup down and leaned back. "I found out a lot about Ella Mae Evans."

The spoonful of sugar that Amelia was about to pour into her tea tipped, and sugar scattered across the table. "You did? That's wonderful!" She gathered the sugar into a small pile with the heel of her hand.

Hannah unfolded a paper from her pocket, and read. "Ella Mae Jackson Evans was born in Savannah, Georgia, in 1809 and died in Covington, North Carolina, in 1872. She had a son, Wayne, who predeceased her, as did a grandson, Joseph . . ." She looked up from her notes. "That was the boy who was killed in the skirmish John and Tom were in." She read again, ". . . and she was survived by her nephews, Tom and John Evans, their two sons and four daughters."

She glanced at Grace. "And you'll never believe where Ella Mae Evans is buried. It's no wonder you couldn't find her. She's buried in that church cemetery where we went to participate in a foot washing when we first got here, remember?"

Both Amelia and Grace nodded. That had been a remarkable experience for them and quite moving, but the church lay in a cove tucked back in a high mountain valley, and they had never returned to it.

"What really puzzles me," Hannah continued, "is that everyone in these parts must have known Miss Ella Mae. How did she manage to keep two men hidden for several years until the war ended? You'd think that sooner or later, one of her neighbors would find out."

"Maybe young men were at such a premium that people were glad to have them around. It was a tough time in the mountains during and after the Civil War. Women and children were trying to scrape by, with bounty hunters riding in, searching their barns and homes and making off with whatever those folks had. I've never heard anything about that part of the Civil War, and I don't recall my son Roger's schoolbooks saying anything about it, either," Grace said.

"Battles make news and fill books, as do generals and politicians. Not ordinary people, especially women and children," Hannah said.

Grace rose and began to clear the breakfast dishes. All those hours climbing hills, for nothing. Her thighs and calves ached for days after each climb, and hot baths hadn't helped much. "We have a lot more information than when we started, and in just a few days."

"This calls for a celebration," Amelia said.

"I'll make a big pot of chili tonight, and we'll have Max and Bob over."

Amelia brought her breakfast dishes to the sink. "How about inviting Pastor Denny and Sarina?"

"Of course. Will you call and ask them?" Grace replied.

"You being a matchmaker, Amelia?" Hannah asked. "I sense that something's going on between those two. Denny's been counseling Sarina since that rat Zachary walked out on her, but Sarina isn't divorced yet."

"When will her divorce be final?" Grace asked.

"In December," Amelia said.

Almost two years earlier, Zachary, Max's son, had packed a bag and vanished, abandoning his East Indian wife and baby daughter, Sarah. Max and Hannah had convinced Sarina to stay in Covington, and Sarina seemed happy living in Max's big farmhouse, having his housekeeper, Anna, available to help with Sarah. Was Denny contributing, perhaps unwittingly, to Sarina's happiness? Grace wondered.

Amelia looked off into the distance. "I remember the day that Zachary and Sarina arrived at Max's house. It was very early in the morning. I'd had rather a sleepless night, and was sitting out on our porch having a cup of coffee. I didn't recognize either of them: Zachary with a full beard and Sarina very pregnant with Sarah. Remember how awful Zachary was, going off gambling all the time? He paid her no attention when she needed him the most." She shook her head. "When I think of what happened in India . . . it must have been awful for Sarina and her family, having to flee their home because in the middle of the night rioters had burned her Hindu father's fields and barns. You read about things like that, the feuds between religious groups, but you never actually know anyone it's happened to firsthand, until Sarina came."

"Well, she's settled here now, thank God. Max and I adore her and Sarah," Hannah said.

"If Sarina were to marry Pastor Denny, what could be better? She deserves a good man," Grace said. "If Denny comes we can tell him about our quest, and I bet he'll help."

When Hannah went upstairs to change, Grace and Amelia sat at the kitchen table. Grace asked, "How is Miriam? I haven't seen her lately."

Miriam and seven-year-old Sadie had turned up on their doorstep almost three years ago, fleeing from Miriam's abusive ex-husband. What a shock that had been to Amelia, confronted with the unknown daughter of her deceased husband Thomas and some English woman. That had been hard to accept, but in time Amelia came to terms with the situation, and Miriam and Sadie had become her family.

"What's new with her and Ben Mercer?" Grace asked as she placed a pot on the stove, poured several tablespoons of olive oil into it, and added a bag of chopped onions. "Keep an eye on these onions for me, Amelia? Just stir them."

"Miriam's been up north to Ben's place, and he's coming back for another visit. She wants to stay in this area, and Ben is considering moving and establishing his computer business here. That's the problem when you go on a vacation or a photo workshop like we did and you meet someone who lives miles and miles away."

The smell of the browned onions filled the kitchen. "I always like the way it smells in here when you cook," Amelia said. "Especially when you bake those incredible sugar cookies of yours."

Grace wiped her hands on her apron. "Ah, for the days before diabetes. Now I use sugar substitutes and watch everything I eat. It's a whole new way of thinking about what goes into my body." She went to the kitchen counter and began to open cans of beans and chili, which she poured into a big pot. "Thank the Lord I feel as well as I do."

"How lucky we've been since moving to Covington," Amelia said.

Grace cocked her head to the side. "You're right about

that. I feel younger than I have in years, and certainly happier."

"The same for me," Amelia replied.

"While this chili gets going, how about playing a game or two of gin," Grace suggested.

"I'll beat you. I always do," Amelia teased.

Grace laughed. "I don't mind. It's fun doing something together."

7

Awkward at Dinner

MAX AND SARINA ARRIVED for dinner, soon followed by Pastor Denny. Immediately after he entered, Sarina grew silent and more retiring than usual, while a flustered Denny spilled wine on the living room carpet.

"If dinner's not quite ready," Bob said, "I'd sure like to hear a bit from one of those diaries you've been telling me about. Would you mind reading something from one of them, Grace?"

Grace looked from Amelia to Hannah, who nodded agreement.

"I'd be glad to." Grace walked to the box beside

her chair near the fireplace, and retrieved one of John's small, worn diaries. After adjusting the nearby floor lamp, she opened it randomly and began to read.

I was a Christian man. I believed the cause of the Union, to hold this nation together as one nation, to be right and just. But, God be my witness, if I'd known what horror war was, the thunderous noise of battle, and the blood and suffering of animals and men, the sheer terror I would feel, I never would have put on that blue uniform. Yet I wonder about fate, for without that experience, I wouldn't be the man I am today.

These days I search and search for the God I knew, but he has forsaken me. I cannot find him in the woods, in the church, or by the river. Prayers rise in my heart, and I cannot speak them. Oh, God, if there is a God, help me.

Lord, I am here, where you placed me, for life is as you set it to be. It is many months that we've been with Miss Ella Mae, and the war goes on. We hear little news in these mountains, and have just learned that in September of last year, 1864, Union General William Tecumseh Sherman captured and burned the great city of Atlanta, then marched his army across the State of Georgia, looting, killing, pillaging, burning, and laying waste the land until he reached the sea and Savannah. The man who brought word to our small hamlet said that Sherman did not burn Savannah. Why, he did not know.

As a Union man I should rejoice at Sherman's victories, but I am sickened by such news. So many dead, so many left to grieve, the land ravaged. Why, Lord, why? My dreams and fears to sleep at night grow stronger with such news.

I never speak of it, the battles I've seen; what I've witnessed I wouldn't wish on anyone. I've heard the noise of war and seen the ground split wide by cannonballs, the bodies of dead men lying in ditches made by shells. One man on the bank, his eyes open, staring, and flies all about him. I turned from this and retched. And battles, all confusion, soldiers running every which way, terrified, shooting anywhere, orders issued and counterissued so we knew not where to turn. In one town I witnessed a house shelled and shelled again, until they carried out an old woman screaming and with one of her arms shot away, and later I heard that the shelling had been a mistake.

That is when I began to hide, which is probably how

I survived to make it into the Carolinas, where we lost our way again, and I ended up in that ditch. Lord, for whatever sins I have committed before the war and in the war, for any man, woman, or child I have unwittingly injured, pardon me. For I cannot pardon myself.

Grace closed the diary and returned it to the box, and no one looked at anyone or spoke. They all seemed to be trapped in the past.

What were they thinking? Had the pages she read stirred fears, regrets, doubts about God, about the meaning of life, perhaps even the loss of meaning? Her heart was heavy with the pain for this young man of another century, and she thought of Randy, whom she loved like a grandson and who was only now and very slowly coming out of that dark forest into which his Iraq war experiences had plunged him.

It startled her when Bob coughed, then stood. "Well, folks. We're here to enjoy the fine dinner Grace prepared for us. If it's ready, honey, I say let's eat." He walked to where Grace sat, took her hands, and helped her to her feet. "Dinner smells great." He looked about him. "Come on, everyone, shake a leg. Let's eat."

They rose slowly, as if needing a moment to shake off

the emotions that beset them. Then they smiled and went into the dining room.

Sarina, obviously deeply touched by John's words, seated herself between Max and Hannah, and avoided Denny's eyes, although he sat across from her.

Usually tuned in to delicate situations and able to handle them adroitly, Grace found herself at a loss for words. Her eyes sought Bob's, but he was engaged in conversation with Max about some ball game.

Denny's eyes found Sarina's, and his face flushed. Sarina lowered her head and focused on dinner. *Yes, indeed,* Grace thought, *there's something powerful going on between those two. He's been lonely since the death of Pastor Johnson, who was like a father to him, and Sarina's a lovely young woman, kind and caring. Just what Denny needs. How nice that would be for them both.*

But she's not a Christian. She's Hindu, a voice in Grace's head whispered.

So what? another inner voice asked. *Sarina baptized her little girl in Cove Road Church as a Christian. Maybe she'll convert and be baptized. Who could object to that?*

It's none of your business, Grace. This time it was Bob's voice in her head.

He was right, of course. Denny and Sarina were adults and could handle things themselves. She realized that

Hannah was telling the others about Ella Mae Evans's obituary, and then it was Amelia's turn to relate her discovery, and everyone's attention focused on her.

When she finished, Bob asked, "So what comes next?"

"We'll try to trace the families Amelia found and see where they lead," Hannah declared.

Later that night, after the kitchen had been put to bed, a weary Grace climbed the stairs to her room. Lights were on in Amelia's and Hannah's bedrooms, and for a moment she stood in the hallway, undecided. Which of her friends did she want to post mortem the evening with?

"'Mind your own business' is the eleventh commandment," Hannah liked to say. That sounded too much like Bob.

Grace tapped lightly on Amelia's door, and at the soft, "Come in," she opened the door and entered a room smelling of grapefruit from the lotion Amelia used on her arms and face at night.

Propped against her white wicker headboard, Amelia sat filing her nails.

Grace thought, *if it were my room and someone came in, they'd find me reading a book. Hannah's probably going over garden catalogs.* Grace smiled as she walked across the carpet to sit on Amelia's bed. "Well, what do you think?"

"Think about what?" Amelia's eyes opened wide.

"About Sarina and Denny?"

Amelia held her hand out and studied it. "This thumbnail grows faster than the others. I file it every few days." She picked up the file that had slipped onto her lap. "They're in love like John and his Jenny. It's plain as the nose on your face."

Grace laughed lightly. "I think so, too."

"Of course, if Denny asks Sarina to marry him, it's going to cause quite a ruckus around here," Amelia said.

Grace knew what Amelia meant but wanted to hear it from someone else. "What do you mean?"

"She's different, divorced, an East Indian and a Hindu, even if she baptized Sarah and wants her daughter to be what she calls 'an American girl.'" Amelia tipped her head and looked at Grace. "Don't you agree?"

"I don't know. Everyone knows what Zachary did to Sarina. She's lived here for two years, and people like her. She's involved at the church, helping with the food on Sundays, and at church picnics, and with the children."

"But she's a volunteer, not the pastor's wife. Wait and see." Amelia filed her thumbnail.

Could Amelia be right? Would the congregation object to Sarina as Denny's wife? Surely not. Everyone liked the young woman. Grace yawned and stretched her arms above her head. "Well, I'm off to bed now."

"Sleep well, and don't get yourself in the middle of this

romance business, Grace. Let them work it out for themselves."

Grace rose and walked to the door. "Sleep well. Think happy thoughts." She closed the door behind her and headed for her bedroom. If even romantic Amelia was warning her not to get involved, maybe she should let it be.

8

The Man on the Porch

IT WAS HARD BEING diabetic—hard living with food restrictions, and awful to think of the effects of diabetes on her heart, kidneys, and blood vessels. Grace knew the kind of food that was best for her: proteins, salads, and fruit; no white flour, bread, or potatoes. Just last month in the market, in the Spanish food section, she had walked away from a box of guava paste—so delicious spread on crackers or bread—shopped for fruits and vegetables, then circled back and picked up the box again. She could taste its sweetness. She had shaken her head, returned the box to the shelf, and moved on, only to circle back once more. This time she added the box to the cart. The result? Her sugar had shot up to over two hundred, and that scared her.

Many times, she had cheated and gotten away with it. What was happening? Maybe it was the new strip she had inserted into her blood pressure monitor? She would prick her finger, which didn't hurt, then capture a bit of blood on the strip. The numbers that appeared on the monitor told her the level of sugar in her blood. It had been too high lately.

She had never really mastered the use of this monitor. When she needed to buy new strips, Grace went to the very kind and pleasant Maxine at the Weaverville Drug Store, where she bought her medication and the blood sugar monitor, and Maxine would set up the monitor for her. Yet no matter how many times Maxine explained its use, Grace failed to grasp its intricacies—until a recent frightening episode served as a wake-up call.

She had awakened one morning with a red, swollen foot and terrible pain in her right toe, which led to a diagnosis of gout. She had thought that only happened to rich old men, kings, like Henry VIII of England. The pain was terrible; she could not take a step without a cane. And for the first time, Grace really faced the dangers of diabetes' side effects.

Because her kidneys only functioned at 44 percent her doctor could not prescribe an anti-inflammatory drug, and the alternate medication made her sick to her stomach. Next came a cortisone drug, which caused her blood sugar to shoot sky high. That required additional medication to bring it down and the continual use of that blood sugar monitor. Today, when Grace went to the drugstore and visited Maxine, she paid attention.

Preferring not to dwell on her health problems, Grace drove back to Covington musing about the letter she had read last night from John to his mother, a letter he had never mailed. *I'm a mother,* Grace had thought. *A letter like that would have meant the world to me,* and she had tucked it into her purse today in case of a wait at the drugstore.

At the top of a knoll, which offered a view of a valley and mist-veiled mountains, Grace stopped the car and turned off the engine. A hawk soared overhead, making wide circles and casting its shadow on the meadow. The brisk wind scuttled fluffy clouds across the blue sky. Lines from a poem by her favorite poet, William Wordsworth, came to mind.

❧❧

Earth has not anything to show more fair:
Dull would he be of soul who would pass by
A sight so touching in its majesty

Wordsworth had written those words about a city, but how apt they were about this place, today. Another fragment of a poem came to mind:

Ne'er saw I, never felt, a calm so deep.

Grace closed her eyes and imagined herself soaring free as a bird, free of diabetes and its dangers. Then, shaking her head, she took the letter from her purse and opened it.

Ma,

My heart longs to see you, to feel your gentle hand brush back my hair from before my eyes, to hear your soft voice caution me as you always did, and which I failed to heed, to not be hasty in my judgments, to think before I leaped. I have learned much since those days, and I think of you when I must make a decision, and try not to rush to judgment. I failed you, Ma. I failed you most by living out my life so far from you, and you unknowing that this life is good, that I am well. Someday we will meet in heaven. Until then I beg you, I beg the Lord, to forgive me. Your loving son, John

Grace wiped her eyes and checked her watch. Two p.m. She had a three o'clock appointment with Mary Evans, a woman who had offered to go through her old family Bible with Grace. Maybe, just maybe, she'd discover that this Mary, who lived in Weaverville, was related to one of the nineteenth-century men. First, however, she must go home and have something to eat. She had forgotten to carry the usual bag of nuts with her today, and she needed some protein to keep her blood sugar stable.

When she turned the car into their driveway, the dogs, Benji and Carole, who had been sitting on the top step of the porch with a young man she did not recognize, rushed toward her, their hind ends wiggling, tails wagging.

As Grace bent to greet and pet them, the young man descended the steps. He was of medium height with narrow shoulders. Lank blond hair hung over his forehead and he brushed it back, revealing large, dark eyes—an attractive feature in an otherwise plain face.

"Nice dogs; real friendly." He extended his hand. "Hello, ma'am. I'm Milo Evans. I teach art at a middle school over in Asheville."

Evans? "I'm Grace Singleton. What can I do for you?"

"I heard you were looking for John Evans's descendants."

"Why yes, we are. Come and sit on the porch. I'll get us some iced tea or lemonade, and we can talk." Her heart thudded in her chest. She needed a little time to gather her thoughts. What should she tell him? What should she ask him? And why, for heaven's sake, was she fussing so about this? All she needed to do was listen to what he had to say.

"Thank you," Milo said. "Either tea or lemonade is fine. Don't go to any trouble."

In the kitchen, Grace grabbed a handful of walnuts and a glass of water, then leaned against the counter and covered her racing heart with her hands. This frail young man hardly looked like the image she had of what a great-great-great-whatever-grandson of John would look like. *Ridiculous! Grace,* she thought. *That is so narrow-minded. You have this image of John as tall and virile, with powerful arms. Why, he could have been as short and slender as this young man.*

The kettle whistled. Grace poured hot water into a ceramic teapot, filled glasses with ice, then poured the tea in. As the ice melted, Grace added more tea, then sweetener and lemon. Taking a small tray, she filled a plate with her famous, now-sugarless sugar cookies, added the glasses of tea, and headed for the front door.

Milo sat on the edge of a rocking chair, his gaze on the porch floor. He started when she pushed the door open, and rose to his feet.

"It's quite warm, don't you think?" Grace set the tray on a table, motioned Milo to his vacated rocker, and took the rocker next to him. "Help yourself, Milo. People around here like my cookies."

He sat, crossed and uncrossed his legs, and finally reached for a glass of tea and a cookie. "They're good," he said.

"So, now, tell me about yourself. Do you live around here? How did you hear about our interest in John Evans?"

His Adam's apple bobbed up and down, then he leaned forward, his palms planted firmly on his knees. "I'm quite nervous about coming here."

Grace smiled warmly. "No need to be. We're friendly people."

"Well," he said, "I live in Jupiter, not far off I-26, near Weaverville." He cleared his throat. "I've been interested in genealogy for a while now, and I've set up my family tree. When I got back to a certain time frame, everything stopped."

"Everything stopped?"

"I couldn't find out who John's parents were. It went from him to Ella Mae Evans, and she was old enough to be his grandmother." He shook his head. "There's no record of John's birth in our family Bible, only his death. It's a mystery."

Grace's heart skipped a beat. Was this *her* John he was speaking of? That could mean that he knew where John lived, what he did, and when he died.

Taking long gulps, Milo drank his tea and set his glass on the table. "This is real good tea. I was really thirsty." He smiled for the first time, looking like an awkward teenager.

"How old are you, Milo?" Grace couldn't help asking.

"Twenty-six, ma'am. I have a sister, but she's a lot younger, seventeen."

"And how did you hear of our interest in John Evans?"

"A friend who's a teacher at Caster Elementary School, Emma Jenkins. She heard you ladies found an old box with letters and diaries of two Civil War soldiers, and that you were hunting for their descendants. She thought one of them was named Evans. I thought maybe we could help one another."

"Maybe we can." Grace rocked slowly, letting her heart settle. "Maybe we can."

He looked at her, his eyes hopeful.

"It would be a great help to me, ma'am."

"And to us as well." She looked at her wristwatch. "Milo, I am so sorry. I have an appointment this afternoon that I cannot break. But I'd like you to meet my housemates, Hannah Parrish and Amelia Declose, and we'll share with you what we've discovered. Can you come back this evening? You can fill us in on your search, we'll show you the box and its contents, and you can see if this is the John you're looking for."

For a moment he looked crestfallen, then he lifted his shoulders. "That would be quite fine, ma'am. What time shall I come?"

Poor fellow. What would be the harm if he read one letter? "Wait a moment," she said. "I'll get one of John's letters."

His eyes lit up. "Oh, would you? Could I?"

Grace went into the house and returned with a letter, which she handed to Milo.

With the greatest care, he opened it and read aloud:

❦❦

Being so far up the mountain, and with three big dogs barking at the slightest wagon wheel or unfamiliar footstep, we were lucky not to be troubled by those who came after the war, selling or stealing. But they came to town and cheated, lied, and stole from folks, and the feelings against Yankees runs high.

I never talk about the war: why the South lost, why the North won, which general was better than the next, the future of the South, and so on. I don't need to remind people I'm a Yank or draw hostility to myself. When I go to town and hear the venomous talk against Yankees, because of Northern politicians coming to the South to take over and run things, carpetbaggers, they call them, I clamp my jaw shut. Sometimes I feel like I'm being disloyal, but why argue, since I decided to make my life here?

There's plenty of reasons to stay. Winters are milder than back home, with less snow and ice, there's good, rich soil and a plentitude of rivers and streams. And when you get to know them, folks around these parts are kind and help one another.

Miss Ella Mae's friend, Miss Maggie Benson, is the only one who knew about us so-called nephews who met up during the war. Her son Issy knew, too, of course, but he's peculiar and doesn't take much to people; he never goes to town and hardly opens his mouth. Miss Maggie comes regularly to our cabin and we carry Miss Ella Mae the bumpy ride to visit her cabin over the ridge.

Miss Maggie's the opposite of Miss Ella Mae. She's tall and bony, with sharp elbows and a long, thin nose, but she's got all her teeth and she's a cheerful lady. Issy skulks about when we're there and hardly shows himself. His name's Isaac, but I've never heard anyone call him by his given name.

Miss Ella Mae told us, "Issy's a comfort to Maggie, and at least she ain't livin' alone."

To see those old ladies sitting together on a porch, shellin' peas or snappin' beans, their hair tucked under hair scarves and heads bent close, then thrown back in laughter over some private joke, makes me feel joyful. I'm starting to talk like I was born here, droppin' my "g's" and saying ain't more often than not.

One day last week, Miss Ella Mae said she and Miss Maggie were gonna take Tom and me in the woods "sanging."

I'd never heard that word.

"Sang's powerful medicine. Cures boils, coughs, stomach troubles, and . . ." She and Miss Maggie looked at each other and giggled, then those two old ladies blushed. Then she said, "It got it a shape like a man, and it done help menfolk—makes 'em feel like they's a man."

Tom winked at me, but it took a moment for me

to understand what she meant. He said softly, "She's talkin' about ginseng."

Miss Ella Mae doesn't have too many teeth in her mouth, but she doesn't much care about that, and she grinned at me and handed me a bucket. "We gonna fill this here bucket. Folks pay plenty money for sang. It ain't easy to find."

"What's it look like?" I asked.

Miss Maggie looked at us like we were fools. "It ain't showy." She held her hands about eight inches or so apart. "'Bout this size or so, and it got three leaf stalks a-comin' off the stem. Flowers come on greenish, then turn to red berries. But it ain't no flowers we wantin'." She shook her head. "It's what's below ground."

"The root's lookin' like a man or a woman, even got what look to be a head, arms, and legs. You got to dig careful, not to break no part." Miss Ella Mae cocked her head to one side and said as if imparting a secret, "I hear tell the Chinese over there." She waved her free hand wide and high. "Mixes it with powdered buck antlers and uses it for powerful magic." Her eyes went wide. "Powerful magic."

Miss Maggie chimed in. "Indians 'round these parts used to call it 'great man'." She nodded vigorously. "Mighty powerful med'cine, sang."

With that, Miss Ella Mae and Miss Maggie picked up their walking sticks and took off toward the woods, followed by Tom and me.

I'm sorry to say we found no leaves or flowers, and we dug no sang that day.

"This is wonderful," Milo said. "I can just picture those two old ladies. All my life I've heard about ginseng and people hunting it. They've just about stripped the forests around here of it. When they tear up the roots, they leave no way to propagate the plants. It's a shame. I'm eager to read all of John's letters, and Tom's as well, if you'll permit me to." He rose. "When shall I return?"

"About eight o'clock this evening?" Grace felt she must share this with the others before giving him access to all the letters and the diaries.

He stood. "I'll be here, ma'am, and thanks for the tea and cookies, and for sharing that wonderful letter with me." He bent and petted the dogs. "I'm off now."

Grace watched him walk briskly to his car, which was parked on Cove Road, then checked her watch again. Goodness, she had to get going to her appointment with Mary Evans.

9

What Bibles Do or Don't Tell

MARY EVANS'S HOME, A small, freshly painted bungalow in Weaverville, was on a quiet, tree-lined street of bungalows, cottages, and neat front lawns that reminded Grace of her hometown in Ohio.

Mary appeared to be past her middle years. Crow's feet about her eyes and wrinkles around her neck contrasted with the smooth roundness of her face. "I am so excited," she said, welcoming Grace to her home. "I couldn't wait for you to get here. Why, it's like a novel. I want to hear all about those soldiers and about Miss Ella Mae

Evans. She'd be kin to my husband, of course, but it'd sure be exciting if we was related. I got me the family Bible from my mother-in-law. She's ninety-five and lives up at Bryan Center in Weaverville now. Keeps it next to her on her nightstand, though she's blind as a bat and can't read anymore." Mary shrugged. "Guess it gives her comfort, having it next to her, but she let me borrow it."

Mary waved Grace to the couch and sat beside her. "Here it is." The maroon leather Bible was big and heavy, its cover faded with time and wear. Mary carefully lifted it onto her lap, then turned the pages slowly. "What was Miss Ella Mae's husband's name?"

"Wayne, and that was her son's name, as well. Her son died fishing in a river when he was forty."

"Maybe one of those flash floods that come rushin' down after a big rain," Mary said. "Rivers can be a blessing, but they can sure be a curse. It must have been exciting finding that old box, and the good Lord mustta meant you to have it." She turned her attention back to the Bible. "You say the soldiers' names were John and Thomas? They're common enough names."

"Yes, and they were probably in their early twenties in 1864."

"Two of 'em, eh? Well, it's gonna take some time to go through this book."

"We may have a lead on John, so could you start with Thomas, please? I'd be happy to come back and sit and do the search, if you'd like."

"Oh, no. I promised my mother-in-law this here Bible wouldn't go out of my hands," Mary said.

"I understand."

The pages made crinkling sounds as Mary turned them. "Well, here we are at the 1800s. Good place to start, wouldn't you say?" She ran her finger slowly down one page and then another. To Grace, it seemed forever for her to reach the end of each page and turn it over. "None of 'em's named Thomas." Then Mary stopped and tapped a page midway down. "1882. I've found a Thomas John Evans died in 1882, but he was seventy-five when he passed."

"That wouldn't be the Thomas we're looking for, I'm afraid." *Should I tell her about Milo, and ask if she knows his family?* Grace decided not to.

The pages turned, and Mary's head bent over the writing, some of it large, some so tiny that Grace would have had to use a magnifying glass. She couldn't help wondering if Mary could make out all the words.

"Nothing yet," Mary commented every few minutes.

Grace waited impatiently. The room was crowded with oversized, dark brown leather chairs and sofa and a plethora of tables, one of which was covered with a

collection of porcelain owls. If there was an air condition-
ing unit it wasn't turned on, and perspiration formed on
Grace's forehead and upper lip. She wiped it away with her
handkerchief. How did Mary Evans tolerate such heat? she
wondered. She obviously did, for there was no perspiration
on Mary's upper lip or forehead.

After what seemed an eternity, Mary said, "Looks to me
like we haven't got a Thomas Evans." She closed the Bible
and clasped her hands across the cover.

After meeting Milo, Grace had thought that this visit
would likely prove fruitless, but Amelia insisted that they
leave no stone unturned, and after making the appointment it seemed rude to cancel.

Grace stood and smoothed her skirt. "I appreciate your
help, Mrs. Evans. Thank you so much, and I'm sorry to
have put you to the trouble. Please thank your mother-in-
law for lending you her Bible. That's a family treasure."

Mary set the Bible on the couch beside her. "It sure is.
I'm right sorry I couldn't help. I'll ask Frank when he gets
in tonight, if he remembers anyone in the family named
Ella Mae Evans or John and Thomas."

"Thank you," Grace said again, then left.

10

Milo Evans

AMELIA COULD HARDLY CONTAIN herself. "He was just sitting there on our porch steps?" She turned to Hannah. "See what I mean about fate? Milo could have lived in Swannanoa and never heard about the box. But he happened to have a friend who worked at Caster Elementary, and heard what we were doing."

"A coincidence," Hannah retorted.

"Does it matter?" Impatience etched Grace's voice. "All that really matters is that Milo might be one of John's descendants, and half of our search may be over." Grace had phoned Hannah and

Amelia immediately upon her return from visiting Mary. Since Hannah was expecting an important phone call, she'd suggested they meet in her office.

Now at her desk at Bella's Park, Hannah reached for the phone when it rang. "Hannah Parrish. Ah ha. Yes. Humm. How soon can you send a man? No, we can't. If you don't get a man out here before Thursday, we're going to end up with a huge problem in the ponds." Hannah looked at Grace and rolled her eyes. "Yes, consider it an emergency. Just ask for me at the front desk. Thank you."

She hung up, shaking her head. "Sorry; I had to take that call. We've had a problem with that aeration system in those lily ponds from day one. So, tell me about Milo."

Grace explained who Milo was and his interest in his family tree. "He's run into a snag. He can't find John's parents, and we know why."

"Did you tell him?" Amelia asked.

"Of course not. I thought it best if we discuss this first, and decide if we all agree to show him the diaries and letters."

"You don't have it in mind to *give* them to him, do you, Grace?" Sitting tall behind her desk, Hannah looked like a disapproving schoolmarm.

"No, I thought he could read them at our place."

Amelia said softly, "I feel as if the spirits of these men have been waiting for us to set them free."

Hannah rolled her eyes. "Why must you always be so melodramatic?"

Amelia looked deflated.

"Don't you feel a deep connection to them, Hannah?" Grace asked. "I do."

Hannah ran her hands through her short salt-and-pepper hair. "I'm afraid not. I probably would have donated the box to some historical society and never gotten involved in searching for ancestors and descendants."

A puzzled look crossed Grace's face. "But you went to the newspaper office and found Miss Ella Mae's obituary."

"I was temporarily caught up by your enthusiasm."

"So, when are you both available to meet with Milo Evans?" Grace asked, looking from one to the other.

Hannah opened her appointment book and scanned the pages. "I'm free on Friday afternoon or Saturday morning."

"I can do it anytime," Amelia said.

"Then I'll call and see if he's free on Saturday morning at ten."

HEAVY RAIN STARTED ON Friday night and continued into Saturday morning. The lawn was spongy. Water gushed along the sides of Cove Road, and cars driving past sent fans of water from their tires into the yards.

"He'll never come in weather like this," Hannah said.

Amelia went to the window for the tenth time in fifteen minutes. "He'll come. I just know he'll come."

At exactly ten o'clock, a figure wearing a hooded yellow slicker hurried up the ladies' driveway.

"It's him!" Amelia moved from a window in the living room to the front door, opened it, and waved to Milo.

Water dripped from his raincoat to the porch floor, and the young man shoved back his hood and eased his arms from his yellow jacket.

"Just hang it over a chair." Amelia pointed to the rockers.

"Thank you for seeing me on such a day." His clear, dark brown eyes hesitantly met Amelia's blue eyes, and his shy smile melted Amelia's heart.

I've never seen him before, yet I feel like I have always known him. "Welcome to our home." Amelia took his outstretched hand. "It was good of you to brave the elements. It's quite a nasty day."

"I like the rain," he said, as she drew him through the foyer and into the living room, where Hannah and Grace waited.

After exchanging greetings, Grace set John's diaries and the letters, tied with a pale-blue ribbon, on a table. Then the women departed for the kitchen to make tea, allowing Milo privacy and time to read John's writings.

Occasionally one of the women peeked in on him, but his eyes were bent to the page. An hour later, they returned with a tray of tea and cookies. Confused for a moment, Milo looked up and smiled. His eyes filmed with tears and he lowered his head and cleared his throat. "Listen to this:"

The nights are endless, their silence broken by the racket in my head, and I can't stop it even though I press my hands against my ears and bury my head under my pillow. The war's over but there's no peace for me. Will I ever be able to sleep without waking up hearing cannon roar and wounded men screaming, and smelling the stench of death? I can't bear it.

At times I think I will end my life rather than live with the night horrors. Many a night I sit up, afraid to sleep until my body gives in to itself, and I awaken to find myself lying in a heap on the floor of the porch or slumped in a chair. Will the memories ever end? And why don't they come in the light of day, when I can meet them face to face? Why only at night? Why don't I dream of home, of the Pootatuck River running high after rain, and the old mill groaning as the wheel goes round and round. There are days when I long for my home, for my parents, uncles and cousins.

Tom doesn't have dreams. He did not experience the dreadful battles that I did at Bull Run, Antietem, and others. That's why he sleeps like a babe. Miss Ella Mae says that in time my dreams will pass and the memories will fade, but can I survive until then?

I must. I will.

At least the days are warmer now. Spring has arrived and dogwood trees bloom wild in the woods, bearing glorious crowns of white blossoms.

Tom checked the plow in the barn. It was old and rusted, so I helped him clean its parts and oil them. I felt useful for the first time since I am here. Miss Ella Mae took the leather harness to town to have it mended. She says a man will come to replace a shoe that fell off the horse last fall. While he's here, we must stay inside and not make a sound. She fears to lose us to the war or to a prison for deserters. Later, when the war's done, she will tell people that we are nephews who found her after the war.

Tom's excited that it's spring and is eager to plow and plant. It's in his blood. For days, he will stand and study the land. He says land is all. A man's happy who owns his own land. Such a thought never crossed my mind, coming as I did from a busy mill and button factory town. Surely farmers lived close by and plowed their fields, but I never noticed.

One day recently, I came upon Tom sitting in the field behind the cabin. He'd scooped up a handful of soil and was rolling it round and round, then smelling it as if it were a flower.

"The edges of this field ain't plowed straight." His eyes gleamed. "I'll make 'em right." Then he looked at the soil in his palm and squeezed his fingers around it. "I'm checking if it's ready for seed, what it needs. If it's heavy or light."

Tom amazes me: to love the land so much, to know the soil by touch. I stand ignorant in the face of plows and horses, soil and planting. I cannot say I want to learn these things, but I must repay this good woman for all she's done for me, and there's no way but to plow and plant her land, to weed and to harvest crops that provide food and security for her. My skills are selling things like buttons and sundries, and keeping books in my cousin's store. Can I become a farmer? I'd be ashamed not to try, and ashamed if I failed. Pa always said I was a smart one. If so, surely I can learn a new trade.

The mountains around these parts are beautiful.

The Smoky Mountains, Miss Ella Mae calls them, and I can see why they got that name, since they're often shrouded in haze. Many creeks run through the woods. I walk each day into the woods, and their beauty and stillness cause a reverence in my soul as if I am in a church.

My arm is stronger now, and I can chop wood myself. I like to bring the ax down hard against the wood. Tom says I am letting out anger against the war, against the changes in my life. He thinks the dreams will soon stop, and I pray that he is right.

Miss Ella Mae goes to town once every few weeks for provisions and brings back news of the war. There is much talk that it will be over soon, that the South has lost and the peace will be signed in Virginia. Tom says it cannot be true that the South has lost. I am pleased that we have saved the Union, but I am a Yankee among Southerners and I keep my mouth shut. There are some things it's best not to talk about.

"John feels so familiar to me, so . . . well, like family," Milo said softly. "I'm deeply touched by him. I want to weep." He pushed the letter away. "I can't read another word right now."

"It's not easy to hear what they wrote. I just wish they hadn't stopped writing. I want to know what happened ten years later—if they had good and happy lives," Amelia said.

Milo looked at her and smiled. "You have a soft heart, Mrs. Declose. My father accuses me of having too soft a heart. It's not manly, he says. My earliest memory is of being told that I wasn't tough. I was never tough enough for my father." There was bitterness in his voice and sadness in his eyes.

Amelia took his hand in both of hers. "I'm so sorry. My mother never approved of me, either, of what I did, what I liked. It's very painful to feel rejected by a parent whom you so desperately want to please."

Milo nodded. "John clearly suffered from post-traumatic stress syndrome. I have a friend who's recently back from Iraq. He wakes everyone in his house at night with his nightmares, and here's John, over a hundred years ago, describing the same thing." Milo shook his head as if to clear his mind.

"The counselor at the veterans' hospital told me that traumatic experiences of war are burned into the memories of some soldiers, but not all," Grace said. "He didn't say why."

"That's a good question, wouldn't you say, Mrs. Declose?" Milo asked.

"Please call me Amelia. And yes, it *is* a good question."

Hannah and Grace exchanged glances. Milo clearly felt a strong connection to their friend. Grace motioned with her head, Hannah nodded, then they rose and headed upstairs.

Hardly aware that they were gone, Amelia patted the chair beside her own. "Tell me about yourself, Milo. Do you have brothers and sisters?"

Milo sank into the chair. "I have a younger sister and many cousins on both my parents' sides. Dad's a lawyer. Mom's from Atlanta originally, but Dad was born here." He looked away, and his hands clasped and unclasped in his lap. "Dad's one of those jock types—tall, with broad shoulders, a football player in high school and some in college. He fishes and hunts. I guess he hoped his son would be like him. But at an early age, I threw away every toy gun he gave me. I'm afraid I disappointed him."

Milo sat straighter. "But we are who we are, wouldn't you say? I love what I do. I'll never make the kind of money he does, but I like the hours, having the summers free to explore new things, and if I stay and retire in the system, I'll be quite comfortable financially."

"It's a good plan," Amelia said. She thought, *I spent years living someone else's agenda, doing what my husband wanted, going where he wanted me to go.* "I didn't become a photographer until I came to live here, didn't become my own person, actually, until I was in my sixties. Goes to show that you *can* teach an old dog new tricks." She laughed lightly.

Milo nodded. "And you had this gift, this talent, buried inside of you for all those years? If I may be so bold to ask, Miss Amelia, are you happy, now that you are using your God-given talents?"

Amelia was touched by his intensity and his interest. "Happiness is such an illusory thing. But yes, overall, I can say I'm happy with my life."

He leaned toward her, his eyes anxious. "So if we're true to what's in our hearts, we're quite happy, don't you think?"

He's obviously searching for answers, Amelia thought. "Are you happy, Milo?"

"Sometimes I think I am. Sometimes I think not. There's a hollow in here." He patted his chest over his heart. "Maybe, as my mother says, I ought to get married. But I don't see how getting married can do anything but complicate matters, and I haven't found the girl I want to spend my life with. And I see how so many of my cousins' marriages have ended in divorce."

Listening to him, Amelia felt as if he were her own flesh and blood, felt that she understood his heart's joys and anguish, felt as if she had known him all her life. This surprised her. It was not her nature to open up to people quickly, or to have them open to her in such a short time.

Milo explained, "I took up genealogy to try to fill the hole. I have always felt that I was born into the wrong family, that some nurse mixed up the babies in the nursery. I want to find someone in my past with whom I can identify—another teacher, perhaps, or an artist."

Amelia resisted the urge to put her arm about him, as she would if he were her son or close nephew. "What have you found?"

"So far I've found a lot of farmers, a tracker, several who went west fighting Indians, a lawyer, a doctor, several businessmen, and a traveling salesman. And now I have found John Foster Evans, who married a girl named Jenny. He owned a farm, but he also kept books for her father at his store. They had three children, a boy and two girls. I'm descended from his son, Alexander, who wrote poetry. He won a contest sponsored by the local newspaper for a poem about love and loss, and they published it. I'll copy it if you'd like to see it."

Milo's face was flushed with excitement, his eyes shining. "When I found him, the supposed son of Ella Mae Evans, and checked the dates, I thought, how could this be? She's old enough to be his grandmother. I could never find his parents, which puzzled me. My gut told me that something important was missing. It was quite frustrating, hitting a dead end like that, but now I believe I know why I did." Milo reached for another letter:

Lately, I can't stop thinking of home, of the Pootatuck River running high after a storm. I close my eyes and hear the old mill swish and groan as the wheel goes round and round. I see the rooster atop the church tower, shot full of holes they say by soldiers passing through during the Revolutionary War. Newtown's an old New England town. Been there a long while, and old families, too, families like the Fosters.

Lord, some days I miss it bad. I miss Ma, and sometimes even Emily and little Iris. Emily must think I am dead by now, and I hope she has a new life. I loved little Iris, with her sweet face. And she loved her pa, though with all these years gone by now, she wouldn't know me if I walked in the door.

Emily's folks didn't like me. I bet they'd never believe it was Emily who started the whole thing, coming after me with those eyes of hers and the way she swayed side to side when she walked. She knew her way around boys. I was just seventeen and hadn't ever been with a girl. Her folks were glad to see me go off to war, probably hoping I'd never come back. Well, they've got their wish.

When I left, Emily went home to live with her pa and ma. They'll have taken real good care of her and Iris, too. If she's still using her eyes and body like she did with me, she'll have found her a man who, hopefully, is rich and can give her the things she wanted.

One thing I bless Pa for. Even when he laid the strap to me after what Emily and I did in that barn, he was yelling that I was going to finish my schooling, to learn to keep books and have a trade, like every Foster before me. After we got married, Emily and I lived with my folks and I went to school. Emily didn't like that. She wanted to have her own home, and a fancy one, too, and now. What did she expect with me so young and still learning? The more I knew her, the more I thought she wanted things to happen as they did just to get away from her folks. They were quite strict with her, she said, watching her every minute. Well, they took their eyes off her that afternoon when we were in the hayloft.

Why me? Why not some older fellow out in the world? When I asked her, she said I was cute and she hoped we'd have a baby. But I wondered sometimes if she liked being a mother, if she didn't see her own child as a burden. My ma was more of a mother to Iris than Emily. Looking back, we were both young, and we didn't know each other. If I ever marry again and have sons, when they get of an age, I'm going to tell them about my past and warn them how a tumble in a haystack can ruin their lives.

After I learned to keep books I worked for Uncle Walter at the mill, then at the general store owned by his son, my Cousin Teddy, selling goods and keeping books. Pa had plans that I'd have my own store of ladies' clothes one day. Ladies always want new dresses, belts with fancy buckles, hats for church, shawls, and such. What would he think if he could see me now, with Miss Ella Mae's son's overalls hanging way loose at my waist, worrying if I'm gonna ever know what a handful of soil needs just by feeling it?

It pains me to think of Pa and Ma's thinking me dead and hurting in their hearts, grieving over me. Maybe someday I can write and say the truth of it. Maybe not ever.

"Wow," Milo said. "That's a sad story. But he obviously started a whole new life here. I hope he loved the girl he married."

"He did," Amelia said. "John fell head over heels in love

with Jenny Banks and she with him, and they were married in a church in Mars Hill."

Milo smiled. "I found their marriage record. I'm glad they loved each other." Milo folded the letter and set it on top of the pile. "I guess back then, you could get away with being a bigamist. Maybe I'd have done the same under the circumstances."

"I think John can be forgiven for making a new life," Amelia said.

Milo nodded, then sat silent for a while. "I know what I have to do. John's my ancestor; I'm quite certain of that. I'm going to Newtown, John's hometown in Connecticut, and find his people. If I have kinfolk there, I want to meet them."

A thrill of excitement ran through Amelia, and she grasped Milo's arm. "You're going to go to Connecticut?"

His voice was firm. "I am. Somewhere in those records there's bound to be someone like myself. And, I'm just plain curious. I want to see this Newtown where he was born and raised. I'd like to see that old rooster. I'd also like to set the record straight with anyone who might be his descendant. John Foster started a new life here. He may have written to his mother, but we don't know that, for he never mailed these letters. How she must have grieved for him. That's a tough one for me to swallow—never letting his mother know he was alive, allowing his family to grieve for him." Milo shook his head.

"He was so young, Milo. After the war, if he'd gone home, perhaps Emily had remarried, perhaps not. How could he take the chance? And then he fell in love with Jenny. If you need to go over his letters again, to get more of a sense of why he did what he did, just call and come over."

"I can't thank you enough for sharing his letters and diaries with me." Milo's eyes clouded. "As you might imagine, Amelia, this has shaken me to my very core."

I like him, Amelia thought. *He's earnest and well-meaning. We're kindred souls.* "I'm glad you're going to Newtown." She impulsively declared, "I'd like to go with you, if you think it would be appropriate."

Milo grasped Amelia's hands. "Who cares about appropriate? I would like it so much if you would go with me."

The money factor entered her mind, but Amelia shoved it away. She would use her credit card. "Wonderful. My photography partner's just been hired by a cruise ship company to teach photography so I'm on holiday."

"I'd be more than delighted. I'll find Newtown on the Internet and share all the information with you. You can see what it looks like! Lord, I'm even more eager now than ever."

Amelia suppressed the impulse to grab him and dance about the room. "Let me tell you what we ladies plan to do, Milo. If we're able to find John's descendants in Connecticut, and we locate Tom's people in South Carolina, we intend to invite them here to meet their relatives and share a grand Christmas celebration. We'll give each family a copy of their ancestor's letters and diaries."

Milo waved his hands and said rapidly, "That would be quite wonderful, quite wonderful! What a fine idea. It must have been your idea, Amelia."

"It was, but Grace and Hannah are excited about it, as well." Then, she asked, "What will you do in Newtown? Where will you look?"

Milo walked to the window and looked outside. "I'll walk the streets John Foster walked. The Newtown Library's bound to have drawings of what the town looked like back in the mid-eighteen hundreds. I'll find his ancestors, and I'll find the man who is, in spirit at least, my real father, and you shall invite all my newly found relatives to come to Covington for Christmas."

Amelia joined him at the window. Lights were on in Max's farmhouse across Cove Road, and through the living room windows she saw Anna chasing Sarah, playing catch me if you can. "You'll find your family, Milo. I know you will."

"I'd like to return another day and read more letters, to get into his mind, and feel what he's feeling."

"Of course you may."

"I'll come back soon and bring you all I find about Newtown. We can sit and make plans and set a date convenient for you, Amelia. I'll find a substitute to take my classes and take a leave from my school."

Milo had answered many of her unasked questions. "How do you do it—the Internet, I mean? Is it easy to get that information about a town in Connecticut?"

"Sure it is. You type in Newtown, Connecticut, and up it'll come."

"I'm so excited, and I'll wait to hear from you."

As he was leaving, Milo said, "I've been immersed in genealogy, and I enjoy doing it. I can probably help you locate Thomas Mueller's family, if you'd like."

"Oh, would you, Milo? That would be marvelous. Down at the courthouse, I found several Thomas Evanses who married within a ten-year period after the Civil War. I intended to try to locate their descendants, but I haven't a clue where to start. That would be so wonderful! Just tell me what you want me to do."

Milo fished a pencil and a small pad from his shirt pocket. "Grace found out that Thomas Evans married a woman named Glory. I'll find him."

He wrote and tucked the pad and pencil away. "I'm honored to try to help find the relatives of Tom Mueller, the man who saved the life of my ancestor."

Amelia walked Milo to the door, and as he walked down the driveway, she smiled. A few days ago she had been adamant about not going to Connecticut. *How fast things change,* she thought. Then she went in search of Grace and Hannah.

11

The Trip to Boone

UNABLE TO SLEEP, GRACE wandered down to
the kitchen. Hannah was sitting at the table,
catalogs spread out about her. "Want some tea?"
she asked.

"No thanks."

As Hannah turned pages, Grace hummed
softly while she waited for the water to heat. She
brewed the tea, set a cup before Hannah, and sat
across from Hannah with her cup.

Hannah's mind was on her work. "We might
have to tear out the original lily ponds and start
fresh." She passed the back of her hand across her

forehead. "I sure hope not. I hope these new people can fix the aeration system, and we'll only have to replace the lilies. I am weary of this."

She closed the catalog. Ignoring the tea, she said, "I'm going to bed, Grace. Tomorrow Max and I are taking Sarina and Sarah to Boone to meet a friend of Sarina's brother Sanjay, who's just come back from India with word of Sarina's family."

Grace sipped from her cup. "I cannot for the life of me imagine why Sarina would put herself through that. What's she going to do? Tell this person about Zachary abandoning her, and that she's a couple of weeks shy of being divorced? She hasn't even told her parents any of this."

As Hannah stood to leave, Grace pulled an envelope from her pocket, removed the crinkled letter, and smoothed it with her hand.

"Grace, you'll never get to sleep if you read those letters at night. You get way too caught up in those men. It's as if they were right here and needed your help tomorrow."

"They do need my help—our help—to find their relatives and reunite them. I'm glad Amelia's going to Connecticut with Milo. Hopefully they'll come back with the names of relatives who'd like to come for Christmas."

Hannah gave a dismissive wave of her hand. "I have

enough on my mind these days, to worry about a Christmas celebration with a bunch of strangers. I suggest that at night, instead of poring over those letters, you go back to watching *Golden Girls* on TV."

After Hannah left the kitchen, Grace read Tom's letter once again. Each time, she entered further into their Appalachian mountain world. Living in comfort, shopping at stores, Grace was fascinated by tales of the travails and toil of times past.

Time's come for the cow to drop her calf. Miss Ella Mae got her with money she made sellin' wood we chopped. John don't know nothin' 'bout a cow birthin' and he stand in that barn door with his mouth a-droppin', watchin' that little old calf come into this here world. Miss Ella Mae, she was so glad to see it born alive, she hop about like she was a girl. John drop down on his knees in front of the calf and tears run from his eyes to see the sweet li'l thing get right up on wobbly legs and suck on its mother.

Then we made us a fire in front of that barn, 'cause we seen a wolf prowling close by the cabin. We weren't gonna let no varmint get our calf. All night, every time that old wolf come close, we done chuck red hot burnin' wood after him with a stick. Next day we fixed the barn door proper and closed up all the holes round the barn that we ain't paid no mind to 'til then.

Now I gotta give John his due. He ain't know a thing about birthin' a calf or milkin' a goat or a cow, but he sure can shoot a rifle. Only rifle we had was one Issy brung us, belonged to his pa. I cleaned it proper, and Miss Ella Mae found us some buckshot.

That Issy's sure a funny one. He'd be a-listenin' out of sight, and if you say you need somethin', couple days later Issy'd come walkin' up the path real quiet-like, carryin' what you'd said you wanted. Never say a word, that Issy, just rest it on the porch step and walk off into the woods like a ghost. That's how he brung the shotgun.

John shot enough rabbits and turkeys that fall to feed a mountainside of folks, and he knew how to catch wild turkeys in a pen. I helped him build a pen ten foot each way and five-foot deep, and we covered the top with bark. Then we dug us a ditch went right into that there pen, and John threw corn in it, and we covered over the ditch with bark. Them stupid turkeys ate their way right through into that ditch and into the pen.

*Come daylight, you could hear them critters flappin'
and squawkin'. Miss Ella Mae put some meat on her
old bones eatin' turkey that winter, and we got to callin'
John Turkey Man.*

Grace smiled, picturing John with a fur cap and a shotgun slung over his shoulders, a string of turkeys hanging from the muzzle. Then she folded the letter and went up to bed to sleep soundly.

As Hannah, Max, Sarina, and Sarah drove through the lovely valley toward Boone, Sarah slept with her head on her mother's lap in the backseat. Max grumbled about lousy drivers, heavy traffic, and having to drive too slowly. He paid no attention when Hannah said, "Go left, Max." Instead he turned right onto a narrow single-lane road, and they drove several miles before it was possible to turn around.

Hannah fumed inside. "Max. Stop at the first gas station. I want to call and let these people know we'll be late."

"I'm sorry," Max said. "You gonna hold it against me the rest of the day?"

Hannah uncrossed her arms. "No." She smiled and touched his cheek. "It's not the end of the world."

Max smiled back at her. They had an easygoing, pleasant relationship, and never stayed angry any longer than it took to realize that they were angry.

Nestled in a bowl of hills, Boone, the home to Appalachian State University, was a booming resort town that bustled in summer with retirees who flocked from Florida to escape the debilitating heat. Max drove along a narrow, curving road up a steep hillside until a huge sign that read Hilltop Meadows indicated that they had arrived at their destination.

Constructed of stone, wood, and glass, the massive house overlooked a lake backed by deep forest. A tall, heavyset man and a small boy were playing ball on the front lawn. They stopped and waved.

"Hello, there, and welcome," the man called. He turned to the little boy. "Run on in, Sammy, and tell your dad his guests have arrived." He strode to Max's SUV and offered his hand to Sarina. "Here, let me help you."

Sarah lifted sleepy eyes to him, grinned, and held out her arms to be taken from the car.

"She's gorgeous. What's her name?" he asked.

"Sarah." Sarina gently prodded her daughter. "Go, up and out with you, now."

"I'm Marcus Stanford." He extended his hand to Hannah.

Max introduced Hannah and Sarina. "And you know Sarah." He laughed.

"My son Fred is a friend of your daughter-in-law's people in India," Marcus said. "Fred's been hiking in Nepal. His goal is Mount Everest, and shorter climbs help prepare him for the big one." He shook his head. "I'm no hiker, and I worry like the devil when my boy's off climbing. The things you hear about those mountains: unpredictable storms, people getting lost or falling off a precipice . . . I've never understood this whole mountain-climbing business." He shifted Sarah from one arm to the other, but she leaned forward and reached out to Hannah, who took her.

Max nodded toward the house. "Beautiful place you have here."

"It's a nice, quiet vacation spot. We live in Ohio, and manufacture small engines for boats and the like." He led the way to the front door. "Come on inside. Magda, my wife, has prepared a salmon salad for lunch. Our daughter-in-law had a meeting back in Ohio and had to fly out. She said to offer her regrets for not being here."

They followed Marcus up the flagstone walk, then up smaller flagstone steps to the front door and into a marble-paved rotunda. This was hardly what Max or Hannah would call a summer home. A curved staircase wound up to the second floor. To the right, through a bank of glass windows, a view of forests, mountains, and lake met the eye.

A younger version of Marcus entered the room, his arms extended in welcome. "I'm Fred, Sanjay's friend. At last I get to meet Sanjay's sister and his little niece." They shook hands all around. "And where's Zachary?"

"He is away. He is hiking in the mountains in the West," Sarina said.

"Mount Hood," Max said. "He's always wanted to climb Mount Hood."

"Well, I am sorry that I didn't get to meet him. Relay my best regards when he gets home, please."

"I will do so," Sarina said. "He will be very sorry that he has not been here to meet with you. This is Sarah, our daughter."

Sarah hid behind her mother's sari.

"How did you leave my family, my father and mother?" Sarina asked.

"Good. They were good. They send their love."

They moved into a room furnished with long low couches and armless chairs. Cubist art hung on the walls. *A cold, unfriendly room and art*, Hannah thought.

"Sit and make yourselves at home." Marcus's deep

voice filled the silence. "Magda, come on out and meet our guests." He lowered his voice. "Our kitchen help quit yesterday, so she's been fussing in there all morning."

Magda was tall, slender, and half Marcus's age. Long blond hair flowed across her shoulders and down her back. If she was stressed, she didn't show it. Her smile lit her lovely oval face.

"We're so glad you could come. Was it a long drive? What a precious little girl." She bent over Sarah. "I adore little girls. Marcus and I hope to have at least half a dozen." She smiled.

By way of clarifying the situation, Fred said, "My mother died when I was ten. Dad and Madga have been married two years."

"Lunch is ready anytime you'd like to eat. Are you hungry?" Magda asked.

"We haven't had drinks yet, Magda, honey," Marcus said.

"Who wants what?" Fred walked toward a mirrored bar at the end of the room.

"I'd as soon not drink," Max said. "I'm the designated driver. A Coke, maybe."

"And you?" Fred turned to Hannah and Sarina. "What can I get for you and Sarah?"

"Ginger ale, if you have it," Hannah said.

"And a Coke for me," Sarina said. "I will give Sarah a taste of mine."

Sarah emerged from the folds of her mother's sari. "Coke?"

"You can have a sip or two." Sarina put her arm about the child.

"Do you go to India often to mountain climb?" Max asked, when Fred returned with the drinks.

"I've been several times. This last trip was my second with Sanjay." He looked at Sarina, who nodded and smiled at him. "We met on my first trip," Fred continued. "He's tried climbing Everest must be eight times. That's one unpredictable mountain. Sanjay and I were the only climbers who spoke English. Most folks managed a bit of English, and one of the Sherpa guides was multilingual. The Swedes in our party were hell bent on reaching the top. One of them carried a lot of heavy camera equipment. When the first big storm came in, Sanjay and I and a couple of Germans turned around. It was hell getting back down to base camp." He shivered, remembering. "I have never in my life been so cold."

"My boy's got the good sense to know when to quit." Marcus slapped Fred on the back.

"Nothing's worth risking your life for," Fred said. "It was an adventure meeting Sanjay and going home with him.

You don't often get invited to visit such a delightful and gracious Indian family. They're great people. I bet you miss them, Sarina. They sure miss you."

Tears welled in Sarina's eyes. *Choices,* she thought. *I chose to marry Zachary and for the wrong reason: passion. My mother warned me, and I have lived to regret it. My father kept saying, "Marry your own kind." But I would not listen to them.* She forced back tears and smiled. "I miss them, but I have a good life in America with Zachary and his family."

This was what she had come for—to send word to her family that she was happy and that all was well. She had written the lie to them already, but this man could say that he had seen her and her daughter and how well they looked, how good her in-laws were to her.

Sarina asked the appropriate questions about her parents, sisters, and her brother's health, then listened as Fred told of his visit to her family home in southern India.

"The estate in the north burned down, but of course you know that," he said.

Sarina nodded, remembering that terrifying night when the family fled and how days later her father hustled her and Zachary onto a plane for America. He was glad to be rid of Zachary, of that she was certain. Well, so was she now. She wished Fred would shut up, but he continued expressing regret at not having seen Zachary.

"Sanjay said your husband's a great guy. He misses him. I'd really looked forward to meeting him. Sure wish he were here today."

"If we had known you would be here, Zachary would not have gone off hiking. He will be so sorry that he missed you," Sarina said.

There was a pause, and Magda said, "Let's go in for lunch. We're having salmon salad. I hope you all like it."

They rose and followed her into the spacious dining room with its long oak table, where they spoke again of India and Sarina's parents. But when Sarina said that Zachary was going into business with his father, Hannah saw the redness rising in her husband's face and squeezed his knee to keep him from contradicting his daughter-in-law.

Two hours later Max, Hannah, and Sarina climbed into the station wagon and headed home. "You're a terrific liar, all those stories about Zachary," Max said to Sarina.

"I am glad it is over, but I am glad we came. Please forgive me for the lies I told. I had to, you understand, yes?"

They both nodded.

"Thank you for bringing me and for not contradicting my lies. It was my pride. If Fred returns to India as he says he will, he will tell good stories. My parents do not need to know that Zachary is gone, or that I am divorcing him, or what I will do afterward—not until it is done and behind me. Then I will tell them that I have made a new life for myself in this country, maybe even in Covington."

"There's nothing we'd like better than to have you stay in Covington," Max said.

Sarina smiled. "We shall see how things will go."

12

Love Comes Softly

SARINA AND DENNY GLANCED at each other across
his desk, then quickly looked away. Since the day,
almost two years ago, when a distraught Sarina ran
down Cove Road and unwittingly slammed into
him as he was leaving the church, Denny Ledbetter
had been her friend and counselor. He had been
the first person to whom she had shown the dreadful letter in which Zachary had informed her that
he was never returning to Covington and strongly
suggested that she file for a divorce.

Sarina's feelings for Denny confused her. *It
is not honorable*, she thought, *to forget Zachary so*

quickly. If he died, custom at home in India would require that I mourn him many months. I would not raise my eyes to another man. But this is not India, she reminded herself. *Zachary deserted me and our child. But would Max and Hannah be angry and turn from me if they knew how I feel about Denny? Max opened his home to me, and he and Hannah adore little Sarah and love me, too.*

Sarina pushed back her chair and rose. "It is time for me to go home. Sarah is waiting for me to take her to the playground at Lake Louise in Weaverville. She likes also to see the ducks swimming in the lake."

Standing at his office window, Denny watched the slim young woman hurry down the path beside the church and turn left on Cove Road, and he thought of Lot's wife. "If she had been as determined as Sarina to get away," he muttered, "she would never have looked back. When will I have the nerve to tell her how I feel?" He walked back to his desk and sank into his chair.

Recently, Velma Herrill had decided that his office needed cheering up. She had prevailed on her husband, Charlie, chairman of the church board, to have the room painted a light yellow. Denny hadn't cared one way or the other until Sarina remarked how sad the room had been before, and how lovely the new color was.

Suddenly, Denny loved yellow. Then Grace had given him a framed print of Van Gogh's *Sunflowers*, which now hung on the wall behind his desk. Sarina had admired it and given him a book of the artist's work, which now sat on his coffee table at home. Alone at night, he turned the pages and thought of Sarina, of how bright and cheerful she was, and the joy she brought into his life.

Denny lowered his head into his hands. What a fool Zachary was! In the beginning, after the letter came, he had felt sorry for Sarina. She was so far from home and with a baby. For many months his work with her had been strictly professional— and then one day he had looked at her and his heart had jolted, and shivers had raced up his spine. He should have referred her to a counselor in Asheville immediately, but couldn't deny himself the opportunity to look into her lovely eyes, to hear her voice and be near her.

Denny clenched his fists. He had been about to tell her what he felt. Thank God she'd left; how could he assume that she reciprocated his feelings? Yet try as he would, he could not banish her from his mind. Her presence at church lifted his spirits and made him a better pastor. People said his sermons inspired them. They should thank Sarina; *she* inspired *him*.

In his first parish, he had loved a girl who rejected him

just when his former mentor, Pastor Johnson, had needed him. Denny had been glad to come to Covington to assist him. When the old pastor died, the church board invited Denny to stay, and now he, a Christian minister, had fallen in love with a soon-to-be-divorced Hindu woman from India.

A knock on the door ended his musing. Ida McCorkle entered, her arms filled with fresh flowers for his office. "Pastor, I brung you these. Got 'em at Ingles's market. They sure got pretty flowers."

"They're lovely, Ida. But you shouldn't be buying me flowers." He stepped into the small washroom next to his office, filled a plain white vase with water, and slipped the flowers into it. Then he placed the vase on his desk. "Thank you, Ida. They certainly do brighten up the office."

Ida dropped into the chair vacated by Sarina and launched into the next episode of the drama in Ida's family.

"June's no-good son broke his parole. He done took some ne'er-do-well girl to a bar. First I set eyes on her, I knew she weren't no good. He's settin' in jail again while she's runnin' with his cousin, Tyrone, over in Marshall."

Sometimes Denny had the patience and time to listen to Ida ramble on; other times, like today, he wished she'd leave him alone with his thoughts.

A while back, Ida, along with many other women in the

area, had been scammed by a charming con man. When the other women at the church meeting had been angry, crying, and sharing their losses, Ida had lied, saying that she'd seen through the man and hadn't been taken in by him. Later she came to Denny to confess that she, too, had been conned and had lost many hundreds of dollars to the smooth-talking fellow who had taken the time to sit on the porch with a lonely old lady and chat.

Her genuine shame and regret impressed Denny, and they had developed a kind of friendship. This summer Ida McCorkle had brought him roses from her garden, and along with the flowers came stories of her incredibly dysfunctional family. So Denny was not prepared for what Ida had to say today.

She leaned toward him and placed her hands on the edge of his desk. "Pastor, I come to warn you. Folks is talkin' 'bout you and that foreign woman. They say her husband's a-comin' back, and you're the cause she's gettin' a divorce."

Shocked, Denny spoke carefully and slowly. "Ida. Don't you remember that Max stood in my pulpit and told everyone how his son had abandoned Sarina and his own baby daughter? How Zachary had sent a letter telling Sarina to divorce him, that he was never coming back?" His voice rose. "You heard him; everyone heard him. Sarina

Maxwell has been coming to me for counseling, just like your daughter May did when she was divorcing Billie."

Ida's smile sent wrinkles racing across her face. "I remember. You sure did help that girl. May's gone to school, you know, and she's workin' at the hospital now." She shook her head. "It ain't right how some people bad-mouth other people. Don't you worry none, Pastor. I'll fix this so as they'll shut their fool mouths 'bout what they don't know."

"I'd appreciate that, Ida." He stood. "And thanks for the flowers." When she closed the door behind her, he thought, *Imagine what they'd say if they knew I loved Sarina and married her.*

13

If Only I Could

"WANT A BEER OR wine?" Max asked Denny. Anna, Max's cook and housekeeper, had prepared a special dinner tonight, and knowing how much Denny enjoyed trout, Hannah had invited him to dinner.

Denny shook his head. He wanted as clear a mind as possible. He had arrived early, and when Sarina entered the living room, his heart caught in his throat. She wore dark slacks and a rose-colored blouse with a rounded neckline and sleeves to just above her elbows. Her sleek black hair hung below her shoulders. How beautiful she was!

Walking behind her to the dining room, he had reached out twice to a wall to steady himself, for fear that his rubbery legs could not be relied upon. Then he managed to pull out her chair and seat himself beside her. Soon he must speak his mind, tell Sarina how he felt. If she rejected him, so be it. He had been hurt before and recovered. No one died of a broken heart . . . did they?

Dinner conversation centered on Milo Evans, the young man who had come forward to ask about the diaries.

"I can hardly believe it, but Amelia's going to Connecticut with him to try to find John Foster's people." Hannah leaned across the table for the bowl of cauliflower and helped herself. "Anna's white sauce is delicious on this cauliflower. The nutmeg she adds gives it such a distinctive flavor. Have you tried it, Denny?"

"Yes. It's very good," Denny replied.

"Milo seems a nice enough fellow, honest and straightforward," Max said.

"He thinks he may have found a lead to Thomas's descendants, someone who teaches at Warren Wilson College," Hannah said.

Sitting so close to Sarina, Denny could hardly keep his mind on their conversation and was relieved when, at the end of the meal, Max asked, "Denny, want to sit out on the porch?"

"I'd love to." His heart sank when Sarina headed for the stairs to check on Sarah, and Hannah placed a good-night kiss on Max's cheek and crossed the road to the ladies' farmhouse. With Hannah gone, Sarina might not come out on the porch. He would burst if he did not open his heart to someone, and soon.

"Max," he began, then stopped.

"What's bothering you, son? You've been distracted all evening."

Denny squeezed his hands together. "I might as well come right out and say it, sir. I'm in love with Sarina. When she's free, if she'll have me, I'd like to ask for her hand in marriage." The words raced from his mouth like lemmings toward a cliff. He could hear them falling, echoing, "Sarina, Sarina, marriage, marriage," crashing on the rocks below.

"I'm not surprised," Max said. "A nicer thing couldn't happen to Sarina or to you." He lit his pipe. "These things show: a look here, a glance there. Best close your mouth, Denny, or flies will get in."

Denny's mouth snapped shut, then he sputtered, "Then, you, you wouldn't mind? You don't think it's too soon? Zachary's your son, after all."

"Zachary was a lousy husband to Sarina, and he's not been much of a son." Max shook his head. "I don't know how Sarina feels about you or about remarrying, but I wish you luck." Max extended his hand, which Denny grasped and shook.

Denny could hardly believe his luck. Things had never come easily to him. His years in the orphanage had been long and lonely.

Still, when Sarina came out and sat beside him, and Max excused himself and went inside, Denny was unable to speak what was in his heart. Instead they chatted about Sarah, who was at that two-year-old "No" stage and getting into everything.

"Yesterday she pulled over a bowl of dough that Anna had rising on the kitchen counter," Sarina said. "When Anna found her, she had dough in her hair, all over her arms, and she was eating it as if it were candy. It's a good thing Anna loves her so much."

Afraid to risk his hopes and dreams by a precipitous outburst, Denny argued with himself, *she's not divorced yet. It's too soon.* He held his tongue, and the moment passed.

After a time, Sarina rose and bade him good night. "I will see you soon."

He nodded. He loved the lilt of her voice, the decidedly British accent. Later that night, he paced the floor in his cottage behind the church. Restless and uncertain as to the right course of action, he carried a folding chair up to the cemetery, opened it in front of the old pastor's grave, and sat.

Tonight was unusually warm for early December. A soft breeze moved through the branches of the dogwood tree that shaded the pastor's grave in summer. A few leaves still clung to its branches. Pastor Johnson had planted the tree, fertilized it, watered it, and talked to it when he walked among the tombstones, pulling weeds and clearing away twigs and fallen leaves.

More than once, he had said to Denny, "I love that tree. When it blooms in the spring, I sit under it, and if I am lucky, sometimes I feel one with it and its magnificent blossoms."

Now Denny spoke softly into the darkness. "Help me." In all his life, he had never wanted anything as much as he wanted Sarina and Sarah to be his family. The intensity of his love, his wanting, frightened him.

"Please give me the courage to tell her. Please, let her love me." He wept then, for the lonely years of his childhood, and for the loss of this dear man who had been a surrogate father to him.

Denny looked up at the three bright stars in the belt of the Orion constellation. "Do I ask for too much? It's not too much to want to be loved, is it? To make a home and have a family? Dear Pastor Johnson, the only father I ever knew, you know my heart. Intercede with our Father in heaven on my behalf, I beg you. Thank you." He lowered his head.

Suddenly ashamed that he didn't feel worthy to ask the good Lord directly for what he wanted, Denny clasped his hands and prayed. "Lord, You know my heart. Please grant me the love I so long for. Amen."

Feeling lighter hearted, Denny rose and returned to the cottage. He would trust that God wanted the best for him.

It was only later, when he lay in bed, that concerns about his congregation began to surface. What would they say or do? Sarina was East Indian and a Hindu.

Then he seemed to hear the old pastor's gentle voice. *Stop. Why burden your heart further tonight? One thing at a time, my boy. One thing at a time.*

Denny sighed and closed his eyes. "So be it."

14

A Wish Fulfilled

EARLY-MORNING SUNSHINE streamed through the kitchen window, warming the room and sending spears of light across the kitchen floor. Denny stood at the window and watched Sarina and Sarah move about the cemetery, laying flowers on graves not visited by anyone else, and his heart swelled with pleasure.

"Thank you, Lord," he whispered taking her presence as a positive sign. Setting down his coffee cup, he opened the door and strode up the short path to the graveyard.

When Sarah saw him, she dropped the flower

her mother had handed her and ran on chubby legs to throw her arms about him. Unable to say Pastor Denny, she called him Padee.

"Padee," she said, again and again.

Denny lifted her and hugged her.

"Padee, see." She pointed to where her mother stood. "Fowers."

"You are sweet and kind to make the cemetery so pretty with your flowers."

"Yes," she said, hugging him again.

Carrying her, he moved toward Sarina, who knelt at a grave and placed three flowers on it. "Oh, Sarah," she chided her daughter, "you will make Pastor Denny all dirty."

The child shook her head. Dark hair like her mother's flew about her face, and she laughed. "Not make Padee dirty." She squirmed, and Denny set her down.

"How are you today?" he asked Sarina.

"I am fine. I want to explain," she said, looking into his eyes. "Last evening, I was too shy to stay alone with you on the porch."

"I thought you might be tired." His insides quivered. *Not here, not now, with Sarah running about, needing to be watched every minute.*

If not now, when? It was Pastor Johnson's voice again. This was crazy.

"Perhaps . . . you already know how I feel about you?" he ventured. *How flat and silly that sounds. Why have I never been able to speak easily to a woman, especially one I care so much about?*

"What is it I am supposed to know, that you feel?" The coquettish way she turned her head—was she flirting with him?

Sarina was five feet and one inch tall and slender. At five feet eight inches, Denny could see over her head and beyond to Sarah, who was picking up pebbles and placing them carefully in a little red basket.

"I love you," Denny blurted. "I love you, Sarina. I would be the happiest man alive if you would be my wife." He had waited so many months, had seen Sarina through the worst of times when Zachary left, and as pastoral counselor, he had listened and cared.

Sarina smiled, then moved closer and placed her hands on his shoulders. "Denny, I have wished to hear you say those words for a long time."

"You have?" Light filled the space around them. He reached for her, and they came together in a warm embrace. "I love you," he murmured into her hair. "Will you marry me?"

She nodded, her hair rubbing against his chin. "Yes, I will. I would be happy to be your wife. But perhaps we should wait until I am divorced?" She laughed.

Hearing her laugh, Sarah ran to them, grabbed Denny's leg, threw back her head, and laughed, too.

"Do I need to ask your daughter's permission to marry you?"

"She calls you Padee. Already, she thinks you are her papa."

He brushed away the issue of religion. How could he tell her that he lay awake at night worrying about whether she would convert to Christianity, which she would have to do if she were to assume the role of a pastor's wife? He wasn't sure what that role was—visit sick parishioners, act as hostess at social functions? Would his congregation accept her if she converted? Of course they would. How could he give them so little credit for Christian charity and good will? They were kind, good people, most of them.

Ecstatic, Denny wanted to shout his happiness to the world.

15

Thomas Evans's Family Tree

"I've found some kinfolk of Thomas Evans and Glory Faine," Milo announced when he called on the ladies several days later.

"Really? You have?" Grace set down her book.

"How exciting. Who are they? Where do they live?" Amelia could hardly sit still.

Milo unrolled a poster-sized sheet of paper onto the floor and kneeled over it.

"Bring that to the kitchen table," Grace said. "If I get down there, with my knees, you'll have to lift me up with a crane."

They moved into the kitchen, and Milo spread

the sheet of paper on the table. "You see here?" Holding one edge down with his elbow, Milo stretched his other hand to the top of the page to indicate two round circles bearing the names Thomas Evans and Glory Faine.

"This is the one." He looked at Amelia. "I am quite certain that your Thomas married Glory Faine." A vertical line descended from those circles to a horizontal line, from which five circles hung like cherries on a tree limb.

Grace placed a sugar bowl, a jar of peanut butter, a jar of vitamins, and salt and pepper shakers on the four corners to hold the paper flat. "I've never seen a family tree. It's amazing." She reached in her pocket for her reading glasses and leaned closer. "Am I right that Mary Jean never married? There's no line from her name."

"That's right," Milo said. "She never married. She was a daughter of Thomas and Glory. It looks complicated, but if you take it slow and trace the lines from each family, you'll see how it runs down the page giving the children's names and their children's names and on and on."

"From generation unto generation," Amelia murmured.

"From generation unto generation," Milo said and smiled at her. He leaned over and tapped several circles. "These are the ones that are important for our purposes. Thomas and Glory had three children: Mary Jean, Ella Mae, and John. Let's follow John's line."

Their eyes followed his finger to John and his wife Arlene Flint, down to their three sons, and down through circles that led from one of his sons, Aubrey. Grace squinted to where Milo's finger tapped the circle. The name Matthew Evans was written in tiny letters inside it.

"At least one of those descendants lives right here in North Carolina. His name is Matthew Evans."

"Where does he live?" Hannah asked. She had been silent, standing back, feigning indifference yet bursting with curiosity.

Milo lifted his briefcase from the floor, set it on his lap, and pulled out several pages on which were scribbled names and addresses: some crossed out, some with question marks beside the names. Two circles were drawn with thick red lines.

"Look here." He turned back to the chart and tapped the family tree about halfway down. "This is a great-grandson of John's son Timothy and his wife Clotilde. They had seven children, and all of them had children."

"It must have taken a lot of time to trace each one of them." Hannah looked at Milo as if seeing him for the first time. "Thank you very much."

"It took time, but it was well worth it. Matthew Evans is one of Timothy and Clotilde's grandsons. He's in his thirties, married with two sons, and he teaches at

Warren Wilson College in Swannanoa, just east of Asheville."

Amelia gasped and covered her mouth with her hand. "Our Thomas's family is that close?"

The chart fascinated Grace. Milo had done an attractive job, decorating the edges of the page with flowers, and had used different-colored circles to represent different families, which made it slightly easier to understand. "What next?"

"One of you should probably contact Matthew Evans and set up an appointment to explain it all." Milo sighed. "At least his ancestor was a Southerner. It caused quite a stir and a lot of resistance in my family when they learned that John was a Yankee."

"Why?" Grace asked.

Milo's hand accidentally brushed against the salt and peppershakers, shoving them off the edge of the chart, which began to curl. He smoothed it and set the shakers back where they had been. "So many northerners have moved into this area in the last few years. They've bought a lot of land and built homes. Every time my father sees another house going up, he assumes it's someone from up north, and he gets upset, ranting and raving."

"He doesn't want them here." Grace looked at Milo. "He seems to be blaming only the outsider. Doesn't your father realize that if local people didn't sell their land, no one could build on it?"

"Of course you're right, but my uncle and my father have this blind spot. They resent anyone moving in here. They resent change."

Grace leaned against the wall, her arms crossed. "Because of the Civil War?"

Milo's brows furrowed; he was silent for a moment. "I think it's not so much the Civil War they're still fussing about, it's what came afterward—the carpetbaggers who rushed in to take advantage of poor folks." Milo looked from one to the other. "Many people up in these mountains had no investment in the war, except if one of their relatives joined up. They hardly cared who won, so long as their sons or husbands came home. Folks here didn't have slaves or plantations. They were simple people, isolated by the mountains, and like Miss Ella Mae, they were breaking their backs eking out a living. And then the carpetbaggers came."

He sighed. "I'm afraid it left deep scars. One of my uncles is notorious for his stories of those times, handed down from generation to generation. He especially likes to tell about a Yankee making off with a cow that was the only source of milk for a family with small children, and how after they took the cow, they burned the barn."

Embarrassed, Milo's face had turned pink. "Who knows if the story's even true? But that and other tales are told to the young folks in my family every Thanksgiving when the family gathers."

"Fanning the flames of old angers." Hannah shook her head. "When is that a good thing, to cause young folks to grow up hating people for something that happened a long time ago?"

"I agree, Miss Hannah," Milo said. "Not everyone in my family feels like that. My mother certainly doesn't, and it incenses one of my aunts so much she won't come to Thanksgiving dinners. She doesn't want my cousins exposed to such vitriol, and believe me, Uncle Alden can sure go at it when he gets started."

"But you don't feel that way?" Amelia was certain that he didn't, but she had to ask.

Milo shook his head. "I lucked out. I got a scholarship to the University of Vermont, and once I left here it didn't take me long to shake off all that stuff. I liked the folks in Vermont." He glanced at Amelia. "My roommate was from Connecticut. His sister, Lori, was my first love." He blushed. "Her father owned an apple orchard. Every fall, we picked and gorged ourselves on fresh apples." Milo sighed. "Gone are the days . . . But there's nothing like an apple right off a tree."

Turning back to the chart on the table, Milo tapped Matthew's circle. "This is a good place to start, wouldn't you say? Maybe he can lead you to other relatives."

"I'll call him and make an appointment. Will you go with me?" Grace asked.

"I'd be honored to accompany you," Milo replied.

"I'll go, too. You coming with us, Hannah?" Amelia asked.

Hannah waved her hand and shook her head. "I think not. Too many of us descending on the poor man might put him off."

16

Matthew Evans

Warren Wilson College, a small liberal arts school, sat in one of the loveliest valleys Amelia had ever seen. "It's breathtakingly beautiful. Look at the mist, how it weaves between the trees, with the mountains behind." Amelia reached for her camera. "I must get out and take some shots of this scene, please."

Milo stopped the car, and Amelia walked into an open field and began to shoot.

"Don't be too long," Grace called from the backseat.

Silently, Milo and Grace watched Amelia kneel

to shoot, walk down the road, shoot again, and then return to the car. Milo pointed to the hills surrounding the valley. "The Blue Ridge Parkway runs along that ridge up there. Hard to see it from down here, but from the parkway, drivers and hikers can see this valley. When I graduated from high school, I wanted to go to Warren Wilson College: they had no fraternities or sororities, an incredible worldwide travel program, and many opportunities for service—locally, all over America, and overseas. My father said that's not what college was about, and he'd not pay good money to have me traipsing about the world.

"I loved Burlington and the University of Vermont. I got a fine education, and being out of the South was, to put it mildly, very enlightening." His voice grew wistful. "But I'd have loved to have gone to Warren Wilson College." He shrugged, stepped on the gas, and they soon turned into the drive leading up to the main buildings of the college.

Old oaks shaded the winding road. Three students sat on a bench by a small pond, strumming their guitars and singing for an enthusiastic audience of fellow students lounging on the grass.

They were directed to the liberal arts building by a girl in overalls with a long braid down her back, and once inside, were ushered up the stairs to an office with Matthew

Evans, Ph.D., Professor of Literature on the door. A departing student, his hair tucked under a bandana, held the door open for them, and they walked into a large room with many windows, a cluttered desk, several well-worn armchairs, and walls covered with books. A man with hair to his shoulders faced one of the bookcases, an open book in his hand.

"Come in," he called without turning.

"Professor Evans?" Grace asked.

The man turned to face them. Bushy eyebrows arched over deep-set blue eyes. "Hello. How may I help you?"

Grace stepped forward. "I'm Grace Singleton, this is Amelia Declose, and—" Grace nodded in his direction— "this is Milo Evans."

"Milo Evans? Are we related?" Matthew closed and placed his book on a nearby table.

"Not really," Milo said, "although it could be that our ancestors were as close as brothers."

Matthew looked from one to the other, his eyes curious. "That's interesting." He waved them to several chairs and took one himself. "You're into genealogy, my secretary said. How can I help you?"

Grace launched into the story of the box and its contents, and by the time she reached Milo's appearance on their front porch, Matthew Evans was on the edge of his chair, shaking his head, muttering, "fantastic" and "unbelievable" and "amazing."

When she finished, Matthew said, "I never gave my ancestors much thought. You sure that this fellow, Tom Mueller, alias Evans, is my ancestor?"

Milo nodded.

Matthew rubbed his hands together. "This is a great story, the stuff novels are made of. I'd sure like to see Tom's diaries and letters. Walhalla, South Carolina, eh? That's the lake country in the western part of the state. I've always wanted to visit down there. Funny how you put things off and put things off." Matthew cleared his throat. "I've had a mind to go fishing on one of those lakes." He shrugged and waved his words away with his hand. "Never got down, however. Maybe now I will."

"We'd be pleased to show you the letters, of course, but you'd have to read them at our place," Grace said.

He nodded. "That'd be just fine."

"Were you born around here?" Amelia asked, uncertain if she liked him.

"My folks left this area years ago due to my father's work. I was born and raised in Ohio, educated at Miami University in Ohio. A great-uncle died and left my father some land and a house in Black Mountain. My father unfortunately passed away before he had the chance to enjoy it, and the property passed to me. Then this job opened up. Six years ago, my family and I moved to Black Mountain."

Grace pulled out a letter from her purse, glanced at it, then said, "Oh, I am so sorry. This is one of John's letters. I meant to bring a letter of Tom's."

Matthew's eyes lit up. "May I read it, please?"

"Of course." Grace handed him the letter.

Matthew sank into his desk chair, opened it and read its contents aloud.

My first summer in these mountains passed fast, and another long winter is coming. My mind goes to Christmas, family, and home. Last year we could only manage to cut down a small tree, since we weren't healed yet from our wounds from the war.

Miss Ella Mae didn't care that it was small. She hadn't had a Christmas tree in years, and she moved her rocker to make a place for it. We set the stem in a bucket of dirt to hold it upright, and Miss Ella Mae was like a little girl, all smiles and laughing and clapping her hands. Compared to home, it was a meager tree in a meager cabin, but the pleasure she took in it filled my heart with a joy I hadn't felt since I went off to war. There weren't any ornaments, so Tom and I cut candles to size and fixed them on the tree, and when we lit them, it felt festive.

We sat around the fire and told stories. Miss Ella Mae can't use her hands any more to peel an apple, but she told us how she used to slice pans of Limbertwig and Milam apples into a big barrel and cover it all with a pan of sulfur. Then she'd light the sulfur and cover the barrel with a clean cloth. She'd check to make sure the right amount of fumes stayed inside, and after a time the apples would "sulfurate" and keep their whiteness all winter. We peeled and cut up apples for Christmas, and they were sweet and good.

Then Miss Ella Mae pulled an old fiddle from under her bed. Some of the strings were broken but Tom strummed the best he could, and we sang old favorite Christmas songs.

I closed my eyes and pretended I was in Newtown, standing in the doorway of our house listening to carolers. And I said to myself, when this war's over and we don't have to hide anymore, if the church doesn't have carolers, I'm gonna make a group and drive old Sam to all the cabins set back in the woods and up the hollows, and sing for folks at Christmastime.

That's when I realized I was looking ahead to a future here in these mountains, and I thought maybe it was the Lord's working that Miss Ella Mae had found Tom and me and brought us here. Maybe this is where I'm meant to live and marry again and raise a family.

But the war's still got me in its grip. The other day, I was cutting down old corn stalks in the field and someone was hunting in the forest. When I heard the shots, I fell flat down in the dirt and peed my pants from sheer fright. This war's never going to set me free, it seems. I was a damn fool to join up. Sometimes, when I'm walking along behind the old plow horse, I stop, and sit down in the big red clumps of soil kicked up by the plow and cry from missing home so much.

Who would have guessed I'd end up learning to live a whole different kind of life in a different place? I sure do miss you, Ma and Pa, and my brother and sisters, though they teased me a lot, and Gramps, and even my cousins I used to argue and wrestle with.

Matthew Evans folded the pages and looked at Milo. "This is incredible. I can't believe I'm holding a letter written in the eighteen hundreds by a Union soldier."

"Yes. John suffered from post-traumatic stress disorder. According to Tom, his nightmares were quite dreadful—not just for John, but also for Tom and Miss Ella Mae."

Amelia leaned forward in her chair. "We're hoping to find the men's descendants in their original hometowns and invite them here for Christmas to meet those who live in this area, like yourself. It seems right to try to reunite the families, don't you think?"

Matthew nodded. "What intrigues me is why they didn't go back to their families."

"In his diary, Tom Mueller, your ancestor, says that he lost his mother when he was very young and didn't care for the woman his father later married; also, that there were many others at home to help with the farm. Miss Ella Mae saved his life and she had no family, so he decided to stay with her," Amelia said.

"John Foster's a different story," Milo said. "He had a wife and child, but he tells us in his letters why he didn't return to them. I'll be leaving next week for Newtown, Connecticut. I'm determined to find my ancestors."

Matthew said, "That letter's amazing. I need to see the documents that led you to me, to be sure this Thomas Mueller aka Evans is actually my ancestor."

"I'll be happy to give you a copy of the chart I made, which brought us to you. It is quite complete, shows where the branches change names and everything," Milo said.

"Thank you, and I'd be happy to reimburse you for your time. What do you do? Professionally, I mean?"

"I teach art and art history throughout the Asheville school system. Lucky for me, they didn't strip this school system of art education."

"So you're a teacher. Well, that's fine, just fine. I'd like to chat with you about that at some time," Matthew said.

"Any time after I return from Connecticut," Milo replied.

The men shook hands, then Matthew turned to Amelia and Grace and extended his hand. "Thank you, ladies, for coming and for sharing that letter with me." He shook his head. "Amazing, just amazing. I look forward to reading Tom's letters and his diaries at a future date."

"Just call, and we'll set up a time." Grace wrote their phone number on a slip of paper and handed it to Matthew.

17

Newtown, Connecticut—
the Dana-Holcombe House

THE FLIGHT TO HARTFORD, Connecticut, was smooth, with hardly a bounce or a ripple. Amelia had obtained tranquilizers from her doctor and dozed most of the way, although she gripped Milo's hand hard when the plane lifted off from Charlotte and when it prepared for landing.

"I wasn't always afraid to fly," she said once they were on solid ground walking down the corridor heading for the baggage claim area. "Several years ago, I went with Mike to New York to sign my photographs at an art gallery. We did that for two years, and then I never wanted to get on a plane again."

"Did you have a bad experience flying?" he asked.

"No, not really. It just got to be too much of a hassle at airports. Once I was patted down. Do I look like a terrorist? I deeply resented that."

He chuckled. "A terrorist? Hardly. I'm sorry you experienced that kind of treatment." The escalator down to the baggage area was just ahead of them. "I've never liked flying," Milo said, "but sometimes it's what you have to do. So I grit my teeth and do it."

Stepping onto the escalator, they descended to the baggage area to retrieve their bags.

Milo had reserved a rental car, and in less than a half hour they were headed to Newtown, population twenty-five thousand plus.

Amelia buckled up and settled back in her seat. "I wish we'd known about all this earlier and been able to come during the peak color season. It would have thrilled me to see fall in its full glory. I miss the richness of a New England fall. The colors are so muted in North Carolina."

Milo looked over at her and smiled. "That sign we just passed said it's only ten miles to Newtown."

"I'm excited and nervous," Amelia said.

"I'm nervous, too. It's all happened so fast. I'm a person who contemplates a thing for a long time, sometimes too long, before I take action," Milo said. "My family teases me, calls me a slowpoke, and I surprised myself being so impulsive about this trip. But something inside's pulling me to Newtown."

Ahead lay a tree-lined street leading into the center of the town. And there, in the middle of the road, just as the brochure said, stood the one-hundred-foot-high historic flagpole of Newtown, Connecticut.

"Oh, Milo, please drive slowly. Look at the flagpole. Look at these beautiful Victorian homes." Amelia turned her head this way and that. "It's such a charming town."

"Do you want to photograph anything? Should I stop?" Milo slowed the car.

Amelia shook her head. "Not now. I'm tired from the trip. Let's find the Dana-Holcombe House on Main Street and check in. The brochure says it's at the flagpole . . . there it is, white, two-storied, Dana Holcombe House." She pointed to the right. "Over there, with the classic columns flanking the front door." Amelia shuffled through the information about the inn that she had printed off the Internet.

"It says here that the design was modeled after an historic tavern, and that it was built on the site of an inn that burned down in 1981 called the Yankee Drover."

After they parked, innkeepers Jane and John Vouros welcomed them into the entrance hall. On the right side of the hall a flight of stairs rose to the second floor, and down the hall Milo could see the dining room with its tall windows.

Amelia stood transfixed. "How beautiful!" She wandered from the living room, to the parlor, to the library, stopping to look at art from Asia, lovely pieces of furniture, and decorative pieces from Greece, Italy, and France. "Where is this chest from?" she asked John, who was standing beside her.

"Mongolia. We have several pieces from Mongolia."

"It's lovely and different. I love your inn and I am so glad we're staying here. It's all so . . ." She looked at Milo.

"Stately and elegant," Milo said.

John reached for two of their bags, and Milo followed him up the stairs carrying the others.

"Have you operated this inn long?" Milo asked.

"We built it and opened it four years ago. My wife and I taught school in Newtown for thirty-five years. This inn is our dream realized. All the gems from our years of travel have found their home here."

"I'd never have guessed it's a new building," Milo said. "It looks as if it's been here for a hundred years."

"That was our goal. It's right smack in the heart of the historic district. We wanted the exterior to look as if it were a hundred years old."

They reached the landing and headed down the hall.

"There was a falling-down barn on this property," Jane said. "John had the men save the wood, nails, and foundation stones. And the wall that separates us from the Newtown Meeting House next door is built from those stones."

They stopped at a door. "Here we are. The Taunton Suite for Mrs. Declose," John said.

"Call me Amelia, please." Amelia stepped into the large, lovely room. "Oh, look, a canopy bed, and the lace is so beautiful." She walked to the window. "I can see your garden."

Jane joined her at the window. "In summer the garden's at its best. We have wedding receptions there." She pointed at the white meeting hall next door. "The couples are married in the Meeting House, a former church. It's noted for the rooster on its steeple." She pointed below. "After the wedding, the couple walk along a lovely path past that old stone wall and into our garden."

Amelia smiled at Jane. "I've read about the rooster. Daniel Cruson, your town historian, sent Milo his wonderful book, *A Mosaic of Newtown History*, and we've been reading it."

Jane nodded. "It's a fine book. People here care about their history and want to preserve it. Dan's in the forefront of that movement."

"I see the terraces in your garden, and I can just imagine how beautiful it is in summer," Amelia said. "I think it's lovely now, with those colored gourds on the wrought-iron tables and the corn husks in pots."

"The corn husks are left over from Halloween." Jane turned from the window. "Let me show you the bathroom."

When they walked into the bathroom, Amelia said, "What a great tub, so deep and wide. I can't wait to enjoy it. I'll be very comfortable here. It's a beautiful suite."

They moved on, then, to the Polo Room where Milo would be staying. "This is great," Milo said. "Wonderful mahogany furniture, and I love that desk. This is perfect."

When the innkeepers left them, Milo followed Amelia back to her suite, where she immediately flopped onto the bed. "Comfy." She pulled two of the pillows closer and rested her head on them. "Great pillows, too."

"I'm really eager to get out there and walk around town for a bit," Milo said. "Want to come?"

"Thanks, but no. I'm going to lie down and rest for a while. Then I'll take a nice long bath."

"I'm off to see the town, then," Milo said.

When he was gone, Amelia sat on a settee near the bedroom window. *So peaceful and lovely.* Kicking off her shoes, she put her feet up, rested her head back on the settee, and closed her eyes.

Before her husband died, they had moved far too many times for his job. She had stood for far too many uncomfortable hours in high heels at Red Cross fundraising receptions, engaged in meaningless conversations with people she would never see again. After moving to Covington, she had donated all her heels to Goodwill. She loved being settled into the farmhouse there, and had resisted traveling. The noise and bustle of New York City had jarred her when she'd gone there for her gallery showings, and after two trips she refused to return. She had developed this unease about flying. Tranquilizers had made it possible to get on that plane with Milo, but she was glad that she had acted impulsively and come along.

Amelia stretched her arms above her head. The faint smell of woodsmoke drifted in, and she closed her eyes. It felt so good just lying there, allowing the origin of the woodsmoke smell to remain a mystery.

18

Andrea Zimmermann
and Patricia Barkman

MILO LEFT THE DANA-HOLCOMBE House, his destination the Cyrenius H. Booth Library. Andrea Zimmermann, the reference librarian with whom he had had several interesting and informative phone conversations while still in North Carolina, had described the library as a two-story brick building on Main Street.

Eager to meet Andrea and thank her for her kindness, Milo stood on the sidewalk and looked about him. Alongside the Dana-Holcombe House, the Chanticleer (rooster) Weathervane, dating back to the 1700s, surveyed Main Street from its perch atop the steeple of the Meeting House. Across the street stood the imposing stone Episcopal church.

Bare of leaves, mature maple trees lined Main Street. Milo felt as if he had stepped back in time. Whistling, and happier than he had been in a long while, Milo walked past gracious Victorian homes, solid churches, and colonial buildings to the Cyrenius H. Booth Library. At the front desk, Milo asked for Andrea Zimmermann.

"She's on the third floor," the young woman replied. "May I have your name? I'll let Ms. Zimmermann know you're coming up."

"Milo Evans."

As Milo walked toward the elevator, he was aware of stark white trim and doors that set off the hunter-green walls and the glass-fronted cases, which held the antiques that Andrea Zimmermann had described to him on the phone.

When the elevator door opened on the third floor, a tall, attractive young woman with soft brown hair and a warm, welcoming smile stood waiting. Andrea extended her hand, which he clasped in both of his.

"I've looked forward to meeting you," Milo said.

"The pleasure is mine," Andrea replied and led the way to her office, where they took chairs facing each other. "Did you have a pleasant trip?"

"Very pleasant, an easy trip."

"And you're satisfied with the inn?" she asked.

"Yes, indeed. It's a beautiful place. I noticed the Asian influences in the decor, and the owners were most gracious. John's very outgoing and gregarious."

"He is, and funny, too. I enjoy talking with him and Jane. I hope your stay there will be pleasant and comfortable."

"I'm sure it will be."

Andrea reached over to her desk for a notepad, tore off a page, and handed it to Milo. "I've talked to our town historian, Dan Cruson, and he would be pleased to meet with you. Here're his name, address, and phone number. Newtown has a genealogical society and a historical society as well, and I've added contact names and numbers."

Milo drew out the letter of John's he had brought along. "Would you like to hear one of my ancestor's letters?"

"I most certainly would." Andrea leaned forward.

"We chose this letter because, in it, John writes about Newtown." Milo laid the pages on the low, round table separating their chairs, smoothed the pages, and began to read:

Some days, when the air's clear as crystal and the haze is gone from about the mountains, I walk up the hill and sit on this rock in the high pasture and think of home. That way, if tears come, no one can see.

What became of my arrowhead collection, I wonder? Tommy Hanks and I spent hours digging them up and finding bits of pottery, too. We gave the pottery to Pa, but we kept the arrowheads. Once, for school, I wrote a paper about the earliest settlers, the Indians, and about an imaginary encounter between them and the first white settlers. I wrote that it was friendly, that they shared the land—but now I'm older, I doubt that was the case. There's always someone too greedy and shoving other people out.

Once I get started thinking of home, so many things rise to mind. Like the time Pa dug out that old rifle and told me that during the Revolutionary War, bands of thugs came at night and stole cattle to sell to the British. His great-great-great-whatever Uncle Zeb and his five sons waited for them and set a trap. They let the thugs go into the barn, but they'd taken out the cattle. When those thieving fellows came out they jumped them, beat them with shovels, poked them with rakes, and took the guns they dropped as they ran off.

"This here is one of those guns," Pa said.

Ma looked skeptical, which raised doubts in my mind, but I didn't let on and listened to him as if he were telling me the wisdom of the ages. Ma nodded when Pa told about a cousin who'd gone to jail back in the 1700s for making counterfeit money, so I was sure that was true.

I close my eyes and see the old schoolhouse, and Miss Pearl with her stick for smacking hands and bottoms. I got my hands smacked one time for pulling Mary Ekert's hair. My body ached at the end of the day, sitting on those buckless benches, writing on sloping shelves that faced the wall. In the afternoons, when my chores were done, I'd sit under a cherry tree in our yard and write love poems to Mary Ekert, but she had no eye for me.

Ma was a pretty woman, her hands soft and her smile so warm. She loved me, and I loved her. She cooked well and baked well, too. I miss her apple and rhubarb pies. My mouth waters sitting here thinking about them.

But there's not much time for remembering; there's too much work to be done. Too many wolves about this year, like the one that tried to get our newborn calf. I must go help Tom put poisoned sheep meat in baskets now, and carry them into the woods to kill the wolves. The last time we did that, we found four wolves dead from the poison. In these mountains the work never stops; yet, there's something about them that makes me glad to be here, glad to be alive.

❧❧

Andrea, who had been leaning forward, devouring every word Milo read, sat back and smiled. "How wonderful of you to share John's letter with me. What a nice man he must have been. I hope you're successful in your quest to find your ancestors."

They talked for a long while. Andrea had been a journalist and was preparing to publish her first novel, about murders that had taken place in Newtown over the years.

"It's such a lovely little town and it feels so safe. Murders seem improbable here," Milo said.

"This was a wild town around the turn of the nineteenth century: White Caps, the Ku Klux Klan, robbery rings, safecrackers, arsonists, hoboes and murderers, and an infamous red-light district. No one seems aware of the town's criminal history, so I decided to create a fictional detective to tell about the true crimes and to comment on the times. My book's called *The Case Files of Detective Laszlo Briscoe: True Crime in Newtown 1889–1933*.

"It sounds most interesting. I wish you great success with the book," Milo said.

Then Andrea gave him directions to restaurants and sights that he and Amelia might enjoy. When he rose to leave, she stood and walked him down the stairs, and Milo stopped to admire the lovely framed landscapes alongside the staircase. Andrea suggested that he and Amelia might enjoy seeing the work of Patricia Barkman, an artist of some repute, whose work hung on the wall.

"Mrs. Barkman's a wonderful woman—generous, kind, caring, and very involved with our state's library system. She has a charming little art gallery in her garden. Her last show was in early June, but let me see what I can arrange for you and Mrs. Declose."

Back at the inn, Milo knocked on Amelia's door. When she invited him in he plopped onto the settee by the window, leaned back, and put his hands behind his head. "Let's go have dinner. Andrea said there's a new Japanese restaurant called Toro." Then he launched into praise for the librarian. "She's a delightful young woman, a writer, and the most helpful reference librarian in the world.

"I'm so glad this town was John Foster's hometown," Milo continued. "I'm thrilled we made this trip." His voice was firm as he gazed into the future. "I'll find my ancestors, and hopefully a relative or two who still live here. I can feel it in my gut." He stood then, and rubbed his stomach. "Right now I'm famished. You ready to get something to eat?"

"Just putting the finishing touches on my face." Amelia, sitting at the vanity, applied lipstick and turned from the mirror.

"You look fabulous, Amelia." He extended his arm and they left the room, went down the stairs, and out to the car.

"After dinner, what say we go to Mocha for a latte and dessert?" Milo asked.

"What's Mocha?"

"A place Andrea suggested. She says it's got great coffee and desserts."

"Sounds like fun," Amelia replied.

When they parked at the Toro restaurant and stepped from the car, Amelia slipped her arm through Milo's and they walked along the sidewalk to the front door.

The restaurant, housed in what appeared to be a brand-new colonial home, sleek and modern, with wood paneling and dim lighting, offered an extensive menu of traditional Japanese and Chinese dishes.

A smiling waiter approached their table to take their order. After dinner, Milo asked, "You still up for some dessert?"

Amelia nodded. After her nap this afternoon she had indulged in a long, hot bath, and she felt refreshed, alive, and ready to dance. "Sounds good to me."

"We're off, then." Milo turned the car onto Church Hill Road, and they drove down a hill and across the Pootatuck River. Milo grinned at Amelia. "It feels as if I've been here before, but truth is, Andrea gave me wonderful directions."

In Mocha, a guitarist's belted out country-western songs in a twangy voice. Amelia and Milo chose a table by a window, drank lattes, and watched the river drift by.

Later, as they headed back to the inn, Milo said, "This has been one of the best days of my life. I like this town. I feel comfortable here, as if I'd lived here long ago."

Amelia rested her head back on the seat. "I've enjoyed being here, too."

THE FOLLOWING MORNING, ANDREA called to say that she had set up an appointment for them to visit Patricia Barkman's gallery on Taunton Lake Road. When they arrived, Milo and Amelia were met at the gate by a slender, gracious lady who invited them into her garden, lovely with rust and yellow chrysanthemums.

"It's so calm and beautiful here. The little bridge and the brook are so romantic," Amelia said.

Patricia led them through the garden to a small cottage, where a large vertical sign Gallery stood alongside the entrance door. On the walls and shelves were Patricia's paintings, in soft watercolors and oils: mountain scenes, sunsets, lakes, and rivers.

Amelia pointed to a landscape of a mist-covered river meandering through the woods. "I love this painting. I'm going to treat myself."

Milo beamed. "It's lovely. A great choice."

Two hours later, as they thanked Patricia and bade her good-bye, Amelia felt a sense of loss at leaving the garden and saying good-bye to this delightful lady and her beautiful work. Once again she was glad that she had come to Newtown with Milo, glad that she had met this talented woman.

19

A Disturbing Perspective

THEY HAD BEEN NEXT-DOOR neighbors on Cove Road for over forty years, yet Velma Herrill had never considered Alma Craine a friend. It came as a surprise, then, when Alma phoned and invited Velma for breakfast at the diner on Elk Road. Velma had hesitated. She didn't enjoy eating at the diner, with all its chrome, shiny red leather booths, and jukebox blaring. But being neighborly and curious, she agreed.

Now, as they sat in a booth drinking their coffee and waiting for the waitress to bring their orders, Velma found herself drawn into a discussion about the letter Pastor Denny Ledbetter had mailed to the members of his congregation. The letter invited them to the baptism of Sarina Maxwell on Sunday, December 18, and announced Denny and Sarina's engagement.

"I don't cotton to havin' no foreigner for my pastor's wife." Alma's lips curved into a sneer and her eyebrows shot up.

Velma regretted coming. She should have figured Alma would have something negative to say. Had the waitress not returned at that moment and set their plates of bacon, eggs, and toast before them, Velma would have made an excuse and walked out.

"Where's the jelly?" Alma turned her plate completely around, then gave the waitress a cold look. "And I'm gonna need a lot more butter than this."

"I'm sorry. I'll get the jelly and butter right away," the waitress said.

"I like to butter my toast while it's hot." Alma scowled, lifted a slice of toast, and dropped it back on her plate. "I told her I wanted my toast dark. This ain't dark."

The waitress wasted no time returning with a bowl of butter patties and packs of raspberry and apple jelly. Muttering about expecting hot food, Alma set to buttering and jellying her toast.

At that moment the music from the jukebox stopped. It

had been way too loud for Velma, and it was a relief when a softer, more romantic melody filled the room. She set her coffee cup on the table. "Sarina's had a rough go with Zachary Maxwell," she said. "How could a boy from such nice parents grow up to be so irresponsible, so awful?"

"That young woman's too different from us." Alma's chin tipped up. "You know what I mean."

"What *do* you mean?"

Alma skinned up her nose. "You know. She's divorced and got her a child, and she talks funny. Seems to me that's three strikes against her—*and* she's not a Christian."

"She's going to be baptized. She's been studying for months, and she baptized Sarah when she was just an infant."

Alma's mouth was full. She shrugged.

Velma had never liked Alma. Their sons had been friends growing up, and she had carpooled with Alma and sometimes sat next to her at ball games and other high school events but with their boys graduated and gone, her contact with Alma had dwindled.

Velma and her husband, Charlie, had discussed Denny's letter and both were happy Denny had found someone he loved. Besides, it was the pastor, not his wife, who ministered to them. Pastor Johnson had been a widower, and no one fussed about that or argued that a pastor must have a wife. As their current pastor's wife, Sarina would probably play a low-key role, and little would change.

But Velma understood that Alma represented a small but vociferous clique in the congregation, and could create chaos. Perhaps if she appeared interested and concerned, she could stave off the destructive gossip the woman was capable of disseminating.

"Alma, if we were looking for a pastor, and Denny applied and Sarina was his wife, would you vote against him?"

Alma nodded. "I certainly would."

"Wouldn't it matter how good a pastor he was?"

Alma ignored the question. "It's a big fake, her gettin' baptized. She won't be no true Christian. Besides, she's one of *them*."

"Who's *them*?" Velma's fingers grasped her coffee mug.

"One of them Muslims who killed all those people on nine-eleven."

Velma sat back, annoyed, wanting to choke Alma. "Sarina isn't a Muslim, Alma. She's a Hindu. Hindus are not at all like Muslims. For example, Hindus are tolerant people. They have a variety of gods, where the Muslims worship one God, Allah, given to them by their prophet, Muhammed, who wrote their bible, the Koran."

"They'll go get married, and one Sunday we'll come to church and she'll be sittin' there with that black thing on and her face covered up like she's hidin' something. And what that somethin' is, is that she's one of them bad Muslims like them people who killed our people in New York."

Velma felt the heat rise in her face. Good God, where was this going? "Hindu women don't wear black robes or cover their faces," she said quietly. "In fact, their clothing is quite colorful. And Sarina's an Indian, not an Arab."

Alma waved her hand. "All those countries over there are the same."

"No, they're not." Stay calm, Velma told herself. Don't argue with Alma. "India isn't like Saudi Arabia and other Arab countries. India's a separate country. Indians are not Arabs." She remembered meeting a lovely Indian woman at one of her doctor's offices. "Alma, did you know there's an Indian community in Asheville?"

"What's that to me?"

"They dress just like we do, and they go to work just like we do. When they have a celebration, they wear colorful, beautiful clothes in wonderful colors, made of lovely, soft material. Hindu women don't hide their faces."

Alma crossed her arms over her full bosom. "They all come from the same place, those people."

Velma wanted to say, have you ever looked at a map, you fool? Instead, she took another tack. "If we object to

Sarina, Pastor Denny will leave, and we'll be searching for a new pastor. That means a higher salary, painting and fixing up that old cottage, and that'll cost all of us. And what if we hire someone with a wife who wants bigger things for her husband—a larger congregation in a city? They'd be out of here in no time." Velma pushed her plate away and leaned forward. "We might could let it be and see how it goes."

"You thinkin' you gonna change my mind?" Alma tossed her peroxide blond head, the roots of which were turning dark. "Well, you ain't, Velma. There's others feel like I do. Some of us think she set out to get him the day after her husband left. I saw 'em tumbling together on the grass."

"Alma, you know Sarina had just gotten that letter from Zachary saying he wasn't coming back. She was crying and upset, and ran into the pastor by accident. They fell, and he helped her up. Max explained it all when he came to church. He explained that Zachary had been rude, inconsiderate, even cruel to Sarina, that he went out gambling and ignored his wife and baby, and how he packed a bag and took off without so much as a thank you or a good-bye to anyone." Velma reached for her purse. She'd had it with Alma. If she sat there any longer, she'd say or do something she'd regret. "I gotta go, Alma."

"Suit yourself." Alma opened her purse, removed her compact, and began to put on lipstick. Then she placed a ten and three ones on the table. "This should cover breakfast and the tip."

Her hands trembling from agitation, Velma started her car and slowly drove to Cove Road. As she passed the ladies' house, she noticed Grace rocking on the porch. Velma swung into the driveway and moments later hurried along the path and up the porch steps.

"Hi, Velma. How you doing? Have a seat." Grace motioned toward the chairs.

Velma sank into a rocker beside Grace. "I've just come from the most frustrating breakfast with Alma." She paused. "You get Denny's letter?"

Grace nodded. "Good news. I'm so happy for them."

"Well, Alma isn't. She's dead set against Sarina—insists she's a Muslim."

Grace laughed. "You're kidding." But Velma's expression indicated otherwise. "Why, that's ridiculous!"

"I agree, but Alma says she is, and she's got some folks all set to object to Denny's marrying Sarina. You think they'll have the nerve to say it to his face? I bet not. Instead, they'll start a whispering campaign against Sarina. Alma's vicious and unscrupulous." Her fists pounded the arms of the rocker. "I'm sorry, Grace. I'm upset and worried. This could split our congregation and cause Denny to pick up and leave."

It's always something, Grace thought. "There isn't a sweeter, kinder, or more gracious person than Sarina. And she's tried so hard to fit in. She had her little girl baptized right there in our church. Alma was there, and Denny's letter said it plain as day: Sarina's studying and will be baptized soon."

"I'm so upset," Velma repeated.

"We have to tell Max," Grace said. "How terrible it would be if Denny left with Sarina because of a few vicious, narrow-minded people like Alma." Anger and anxiety swept through her. "It would hurt Max and Hannah, too. They love Sarina and that grandbaby of theirs."

Grace laid her hand on Velma's arm. "Would it help if Max delivered a talk on tolerance at church? The talk he gave after Zachary left squelched those nasty rumors circulating about Denny and Sarina. And I bet Alma was behind those rumors, too. What makes her so nasty?"

"I don't know why she's like this." Velma shook her head. "As far back as I recall, she's always been a gossip and troublemaker, but this is the worst." She gave the rocker a vigorous shove. "I've never seen Alma so stirred up about anything, or so mean. She's so fixed in her mind that Sarina's a Muslim, and that Indians and Arabs are alike."

"This ought to be a happy time for Sarina," Grace said, "especially after all she's been through since coming to Covington. Even if Alma and her group fail to sway others, imagine how it would be for Sarina, knowing that some of the congregation don't want her. Denny will leave us."

Velma gave Grace a speculative look. "I wonder if I could get my Charlie to talk to Frank. Charlie says Frank's the only one who can shut Alma up."

"Did Alma mention how Frank feels about Denny and Sarina?" Grace asked.

"No, she didn't. I bet she never showed Frank the letter." Velma was silent for a moment. "Charlie considers Frank a reasonable, fair-minded person. Maybe if he talked to him, Frank could nip this in the bud." Velma sighed. "I feel a whole heap better, now that we talked. I agree with you, Grace. We gotta do something, and not let Alma hurt Sarina and drive Denny away."

Velma walked to the steps. "Ever wonder what it would be like to change your religion, especially to one that's so different? I always wonder about Christians who become Muslims. They say some Christians are doing that right here in North Carolina. Why would they?"

"Beats me," Grace said.

Velma lingered at the top of the steps. "Maybe folks who

change their religion become real disillusioned with what they have. I wouldn't change my religion."

"Maybe Alma doesn't know that it was Muslims who burned Sarina's father's fields, or that her family fled for their lives in the middle of the night. That's why she and Zachary came to America," Grace said.

"I wonder if it would make any difference, her knowing that?" Velma went down the steps.

Grace watched her car drive away. Across the road, Anna and Sarah were playing in Max's yard. *Sarah will be bilingual,* Grace thought. *Anna speaks to her in Spanish.* She remembered that Brenda Tate, the principal of Caster Elementary School and her good friend, had told her recently that she'd hired a Spanish teacher for the fourth and fifth grades starting in the fall. *No harm in being fluent in more than one language. Sarah will be ahead of the game by the time she enters fourth grade. If she's still living in Covington.* Grace felt a pang in her heart.

Grace pulled her new cell phone from her pocket. Carefully, she punched in Bob's phone number, and hit Send.

"Hi, honey," Bob said.

"How'd you know it was me?"

"Caller ID. Your phone has it, too; all cell phones do now."

"We have a problem. Can you come over?"

"You're not sick?" His voice was concerned.

"No, I'm fine. It's about Denny and Sarina."

"Be right over."

GRACE LOOKED OUT THE kitchen window and watched Bob dash from his car. It had begun to rain, and she handed him a towel at the front door and ushered him into the kitchen.

Bob slid his arm around her shoulder. "Now tell me, honey, what's happened?"

"Alma Craine's gossiping and troublemaking." She related Velma's story.

"That's ridiculous. They can't control whom Denny marries," Bob snapped.

"But Alma and her cronies can make things really unpleasant for them, especially Sarina, and Denny will leave."

"That's true." Bob was silent for a moment.

"Alma has it in her head that Sarina's a Muslim. She doesn't know the difference between a Hindu and a Muslim, and I doubt she'd read a single book or even an article to find out."

Bob shook his head. "Stupid woman."

"Velma's going to ask Charlie to talk to Frank; maybe

Frank can stop his wife. I thought if you and Max let Charlie know you're behind him, it would help."

"That's really interfering, don't you think?"

"It would be much worse if Alma spread vicious stories about Sarina, and got other people stirred up about her being a Muslim. Next thing, Alma will have it that Sarina's father or her brothers were in on the plot to blow up the Twin Towers."

"That's sheer nonsense." Bob drummed his fingers on the table. "But I see your point. Let's go to Bella's Park and find Max. I don't make light of the harm an inveterate troublemaker like Alma can do."

20

Moving On

MAX STRETCHED, AWAKENING FROM a nap on the couch in Hannah's office. Turning his head, he could see Hannah busy at her desk. Lord, he loved that woman. Several years ago, when his wife Bella passed away after a long illness, he had decided never to risk the terrible pain of losing someone he loved again. But as he worked with the strong-minded and independent Hannah, so different from Bella, he had unwittingly fallen in love with her. And here they were, married for almost three years and working amicably together. They even had a lovely daughter-in-law and a granddaughter whom they both adored.

As for his errant son, Zachary had demanded Max give him land on which he would build a housing development—the very thing Max had bought the land to prevent! When Max refused, Zachary had cursed at him. In those months prior to the birth of his daughter, after bringing his wife from her home in India, his son had ignored his pregnant wife, and even after Sarah was born, he continued to treat her with indifference. It had been painful for them all, dealing with Zachary, but they were all well rid of him.

Sensing that he was awake, Hannah looked up from her work. She had replaced the love seat with this couch expressly so that Max could sneak away and rest. Lately he'd been more tired than usual, and resting in his own office, which was close to the receptionist area, proved to be impossible since the staff had no compunction about walking in at will. Initially Max had encouraged this open door policy, but things had changed. Now he was older and needed these little naps to keep him going, and no one intruded on Hannah. Even Grace and Amelia called ahead.

"Have a good rest? I wish I could lie down and drift off the way you can," Hannah said.

"I've got a clear conscience," Max teased.

"You work too hard for a man of eighty."

"Eighty? I can't be eighty. Most of the time I feel sixty-five."

This was not true. Lately he'd started feeling his age, and it was hard to accept, hard to admit, even to himself. Max swung his long legs over the edge of the couch and sat up.

"Where do the years go? One day you're young, the next you're middle aged, and suddenly you're eighty." His voice grew hoarse with emotion. "I could handle being seventy, but being eighty's harder."

Hannah leaned forward, her elbows on the desk, her chin on her hands. "You're a basically healthy man, and you come from a long-lived family. What was your father, ninety-three when he died?"

Max nodded.

Hannah continued. "I used to think about dying, about no longer being in the world, and think what a shame for me to be dead. I have so much to offer, so much to live for." She laughed. "Then one day I sat down and listed a half-dozen geniuses: Einstein, Salk, Shakespeare. They made really important contributions to the world. Who am I to fuss about dying? When my time's up, it's up."

"I wonder what your geniuses thought about dying?"

Max said. "I sure wish someone had interviewed them and written a book about their feelings. I bet a lot of them felt the way you do and had trouble coming to terms with it."

Hannah sat back. "Why are we talking about dying?" A knock on the office door silenced Hannah. She straightened her shoulders. "Come in."

Bob and Grace set dripping umbrellas in the hall and stepped into the office.

Bob and Grace together and in the rain, Hannah thought. *Something serious must have happened.*

Grace immediately related the problem with Alma, then Velma's plan to put a stop to the gossip.

"Frank's the answer," Max said. "He's a reasonable man and well aware of the . . . foibles of his wife."

Calls were made to Charlie then, and their concerns expressed. Velma had spoken to him, he said, and he would contact Frank. Could he set up a meeting in the conference room at Bella's Park? He asked Max and Bob to attend that meeting, and they agreed to be there.

That settled, their talk turned to Amelia. "Have you heard from her or Milo?" Grace asked Hannah.

"Let me check the answering service." Hannah picked up the phone, reached for a pencil, wrote, and hung up. "It was Amelia. She left a message and the phone number of the inn where they're staying in Newtown. They were going out to see the town and have lunch." Hannah looked at Grace. "She's probably left a message at home as well."

"I preferred my old sit-on-the-table answering machine." Grace looked accusingly at Bob, who had insisted that she switch to an answering service. "It had a light that blinked. Half the time I forget to pick up the phone to check for messages, and it's a surprise when I do pick up to call someone and there's this beep, beep, beep." She gave Bob a disgruntled look, to which he lifted his arms and shrugged. "I'll check when I get home," Grace said. "Give me that number, just in case she didn't call home."

Hannah wrote the number on a slip of paper and handed it to Grace.

IT WAS PAST FOUR o'clock when Grace reached Amelia, who raved about the bathtub, how deep and wide it was, how the hot water kept coming. "Why don't we have a huge tub like that? We could have one installed, couldn't we? Grace, you'd love it. I must have spent an hour in that tub. We ran around, talking with people and I was aching everywhere when I got home, but after soaking in that tub, every cranky bone in my body is soothed."

"Sounds like you're having a great time."

Amelia's voice grew serious. "This town is utterly charming, Grace. If I didn't love you so much and my life in Covington, I'd move here in a minute. You wouldn't believe this flagpole stuck smack in the center of their Main Street. The Dana-Holcombe House is right close by it. The street's beautiful—blocks and blocks of gorgeous Victorian houses, old maple trees that must be gorgeous in summer when they are thick with foliage, and the colonial architecture! People have lived here since before the Revolutionary War. The town's over three hundred years old.

"Andrea Zimmermann, the reference librarian, has been incredibly helpful to Milo. She's directed him to the town historian, and they've got a genealogical society and a genealogical club. Milo thinks he's died and gone to heaven," Amelia said. "He's like a little boy, running from meeting to meeting, talking to people. He's getting his ancestors' chart organized, and he thinks there are relatives living in a place nearby called Sandy Hook, where there used to be a huge gristmill." She paused. "You there, Grace?"

"I sure am. It sounds great, all of it, and a most productive time for Milo."

"Yes, it is. It's been wonderful. I am so glad I came along. I hope you and Hannah are having luck getting information about Tom's family in Walhalla." Amelia giggled like a schoolgirl. "I don't think you'll find a tub like this one down in Walhalla, though. There's Milo at the door. We're off to have coffee at Mocha. You'd love this place, Grace, it's really fun. And they have caramel-flavored drinks on their menu."

"Enjoy yourself. Give Milo my best regards."

Well, Grace thought as she hung up the phone, *Milo seems to have hit the jackpot, and Amelia's enjoying herself. Hannah and I haven't made a move to check out Tom's people in Walhalla.* She looked at the calendar on the wall: Time was of the essence.

That evening, after dinner at the ladies' farmhouse, Grace told Bob, Hannah, and Max about Amelia's phone call.

"They haven't let any grass grow under their feet, now, have they?" Max patted his stomach. "I ate too much. You're too good a cook, Grace." His eyes met Hannah's. "You ladies need a little help getting started in Walhalla? I'll drive you down on Friday, if you'd like. We could have lunch at the Steak House Cafeteria, mosey on over to the courthouse, and inquire about early pioneer days. Settled by Germans, I believe it was. Shouldn't be hard to find Tom Mueller's ancestors."

Grace heaved a sigh of relief. She dreaded making the round trip to South Carolina alone. Bob was busy with golf, and Hannah gave no indication that she was interested in pursuing this, although they had agreed to take on the project.

"That sounds great." Hannah directed her gaze at Grace across the table. "Friday all right with you?"

Grace suppressed her annoyance. It was Hannah who had kept putting this off. "Friday's fine. Thanks for driving us, Max."

Max shoved back his chair. "We'll get an early start, say, nine?"

Both women nodded. But first there was the meeting tomorrow with the men and Frank. Grace couldn't wait for it to be over, and for Bob to bring news of what had taken place. She hoped Frank would be willing and able to control Alma. And then Grace, worrier that she was, worried that Denny or Sarina would get word of Alma's doings before Frank could intervene.

Grace wondered why Alma gossiped, why she enjoyed slamming a stone into placid waters. She avoided Alma. Anybody with good sense would. But maybe that wasn't such a good idea. Maybe Alma gossiped to get attention. Grace shook her head. *I'm going around and around in circles. I have no idea why anyone does what they do.*

IT WAS FIVE IN the afternoon when Bob's car pulled into the ladies' driveway. Watching him from the kitchen window, Grace's heart sank. He was dawdling, taking time to check a rear tire. Now he was coming up the steps way too slowly. Why would he procrastinate, unless he had bad news?

Grace picked up a dirty glass in the sink, rinsed it, and set it in the dishwasher. She wiped her hands on a checkered dishcloth, took a deep breath, and turned to face Bob as he entered the kitchen. "How'd it go?"

Bob pulled out a chair at the table, sank into it, looked up at her, and grinned. "Pretty darn good, considering."

"Now, what does that mean?"

Bob reminded her of a boy who'd succeeded in pulling off a fairly harmless prank, but a prank, nevertheless. Grace slapped him on the shoulder with the dish towel. "Why do I always fall for your tricks? You figured I'd be watching you out of the window, didn't you?" She sat in the chair across from him.

"Yep." His face grew serious. He removed his sunglasses and lay them on the table. "Frank likes Sarina, thinks she's a fine young woman who got a really bum deal. He hadn't heard a word about Denny and Sarina's engagement or her baptism." His eyebrows shot up. "Apparently, Alma *forgot* to show him Denny's letter.

"Anyway, Charlie put it that we all like Pastor Denny,

and Frank agreed that he hoped he'd stay on here as pastor. Charlie said we'd have a better chance of keeping Denny if he married Sarina, and that Denny, being a young man, sooner or later would want a wife and he might just find a girl who'd prefer a bigger parish with more money, and that sort of thing. Sarina's happy here and considers Max and Hannah and all of us family."

"And that worked?"

"Yes, it did. Frank agreed with Charlie, and then Max and I agreed with Frank."

Grace could contain her impatience no longer. "So what's Frank going to do? He can't watch Alma day and night."

"Frank assured us that he'd take care of it—whatever that means. We'll have to trust that he knows what he's about, and Alma's revolt will die down." Bob's brows drew together. "Honey, none of us really knows what's between a couple, and certainly not those of us who've come here from somewhere else. Charlie said that Frank has his ways. Who am I to question?"

Grace went to the stove and turned on the oven. "I've got a chicken casserole going in this oven in a few minutes. It's a new recipe. I hope it's good." She returned to Bob, bent, and kissed his cheek. "Thanks, Bob. I'm sorry to get you involved in this. I know you hate it."

"Truth is, I didn't do much more than watch."

"I'm sure it helped that you and Max were there to back up Charlie."

"What did you do today?" Bob crossed his arms over his chest.

"Not much, I'm afraid."

"Well," Bob said, "I called the clerk at the courthouse in Walhalla. Seems that in 1849, a group of German immigrants living in Georgia bought a huge tract of land there, and in 1850 they named the town Walhalla, which means 'paradise' or 'garden of the gods.' They were a community of farmers, mainly, and I imagine it would seem like paradise to them: rolling land, rich soil, mild winters compared to the winters in Germany. There were several Muellers among the founding fathers, so she thought it would be fairly easy to trace your Tom's ancestors."

Reaching across the table, Bob rested his hands on Grace's. "It's gonna be hard for Max to take Friday off to drive you gals to Walhalla, and Hannah needs to be at this meeting they're having at Bella's Park. Max felt bad about it, but you know things come up when you're trying to run a business. So I'll be glad to drive you down."

Grace leaned forward. "That would be great, but what about your golf game and Martin?"

"I can always golf, and Martin's got other people he can team with. I talked to him. It's okay."

Grace smiled. "You're a sweetheart, Bob, and I love you."

Bob held her hands in his. "I'd like to do this with you, honey—just the two of us. It'll be nice." He was silent a moment, "Have you heard from Amelia again?"

Grace nodded. "Amelia and Milo are making good headway in Newtown. Seems his family goes back a long way there. Milo's found an ancestor, Frederick Evans Nikelson, a teacher and an actor in local productions, the kind of man Milo had hoped to find. He's one of the few relatives on his family tree who wasn't a farmer, a worker in or owner of a button factory, a worker at a mill, or a county employee."

Her brows drew together. "You'd think Milo would realize that many men who farmed to feed their families back then might also have had the hearts of poets. Maybe they wrote love poems to their girlfriends or wives, or stopped plowing to admire a sunset."

Bob scratched his head, his mind no longer on Milo. "I was thinking, Grace. How about we ask Roger to do a little legwork for us at the Walhalla courthouse? It would save time and he lives in Salem. What's that, twenty minutes to Walhalla?"

"Yes."

"He could check out those old birth, marriage, and death records; see if he can identify your Tom Mueller's family. It might narrow the search and save us a lot of time. Does your Thomas say how old he is in any of his diaries? It would help if you could give Roger a range of ages or dates."

The oven beeped, indicating it had reached the desired temperature and Grace slipped the casserole into the oven. "That's a great idea. I thought about asking Roger to meet us in Walhalla at The Steak House for lunch, but then I worried—he's got his little tree business, and I know it takes a lot of his time."

"There's no such thing as a little business. Big or small, business consumes you. Remember our *little* Cottage Tearoom? It nearly killed us—on our feet too much, worrying about keeping the books right, taxes to pay, and on and on."

Grace nodded. "It was fun for a while, but I agree. That tearoom wasn't the right thing for us at our ages. I was happy when we sold it." Her brow wrinkled as she thought. "Bob, do you realize what you've just said—'on your feet too much'? You walk for hours on a golf course. Why isn't that exhausting?"

"Well, the grass is easier on the back and feet. But you're right, it can be quite exhausting. Some days I come home, run hot water in the tub, and soak my feet." He shook his head. "I love golf, getting out in the fresh air, the companionship of fellow golfers. I'd better not complain about aching feet, or you'll be after me to cut back."

"You could use a golf cart."

"Golf carts are for sissies." He smiled at her. "But maybe one of these days I'll start using one."

"Meanwhile, you'll have aching feet. You men." She laughed.

"Each time I hit that ball, it's a whole new adventure."

"I guess so, since so many people enjoy it." Hands on hips, she looked down at him. "So about Tom Mueller and Walhalla, I'll see if Roger can help. I'm happy it'll be just the two of us going. We haven't been away alone for a long time."

Bob played with the stems of his sunglasses, closing and opening them. "Let me call your son and see what his schedule's like, and we'll work out a time to go down there."

"Thanks, Bob, you're a dear. You staying for dinner? I know chicken isn't your favorite."

He shrugged. "I enjoy anything you cook. I'll go home, take a shower, and be back about six."

21

A Time and Place

✦ ✦

"WHERE WOULD YOU LIKE to be married, and when?" Denny asked.

Sarina studied him, a whimsical smile spreading across her face. "In your church, of course." She shook her head. "But why are we talking about the wedding when I am not as yet baptized?"

Denny stirred his iced tea. "You'll learn what you need to know fast. In a month you'll be ready for baptism."

"How is that possible? I have to learn so much about a new and different religion." She bit her lower lip, then shrugged. "Hannah and the ladies would like to have an engagement party for us, and I have some weeks for learning before my baptism. It will be the next year before we can make a date to be married."

"I'd hoped we could be married this year, somewhere about Christmas," he replied.

Sarina walked behind his chair and rested her hands on his shoulders. "Dear Denny. I love you, but you are so impatient. If the ladies find the ancestors and descendants of their soldiers, there will be a great and important celebration at Christmas. It is not the time to add another celebration to distract from their gathering of the relatives."

Reaching up, Denny placed his hands over hers. It always amazed him how small and soft they were. He loved holding them, touching her slender, tapered fingers. "I *am* impatient, yes. It seems that I've waited for you all my life."

She bent and kissed his cheek. "Also we must consider your congregation. It is important that you prepare them. They have had you all to themselves; they are not used to sharing you with a wife. Pastor Johnson was not married, so they have not had a pastor's wife for a long time. They will need to get used to that idea."

Grasping her hand, Denny pulled Sarina gently around the chair and into his lap. "You're wise to think about all of this, and kind to consider their feelings. You'll be a wonderful pastor's wife, Sarina. I'm the luckiest man in the world."

"At my baptism and to our wedding, no one must be left out. We must make them all feel that they are important to us, and to you, especially." She pulled away from him and clasped her hands, a look of desolation in her eyes. "What of my parents? How can I marry without inviting them to my wedding? I must tell them that I am divorced, that I have been lying to them all this time. It does not pay to lie, I will never tell a lie to anyone again.

"My father used to say to us, 'A lie is like wet manure: you walk in it and you will stink.'" She walked around his desk and faced Denny. "What will I do? We cannot marry without inviting them." Sarina paced the narrow space from his desk to the window and back. "They will not come, but we must invite them," she said. "This very day I must write my mother." She turned worried eyes to Denny. "I will be a Christian, and I will wear a white dress as is your custom. At home I would wear a red sari and headdress, paint my hands with henna, and braid my hair." Tears filled her eyes and she sank into a chair and rested her head in her hands on Denny's desk. "It is so different in America. My parents will never understand."

Denny came around the desk, bent and took her face in his hands, and kissed her forehead. "My dearest love. I know how hard it will be for you to tell them about Zachary—how he treated you and his leaving. But they'll be glad about Max and Hannah. Your parents cannot help but love them for the way they love you, and how they have cared for you and Sarah."

"My father never liked Zachary." Tears fell down her cheeks and Denny wiped them away.

"It's all right, Sarina. You decide what you want to do, and I'll help in any way I can. Would you like to phone your parents?" If it would relieve her mind and end the guilt she carried, that was all that mattered.

Sarina shook her head. "It will cost too much money. I would not take advantage of Max's goodness or of yours. No, I will write to my mother."

"Letters will take a long time to go and come. Talk to them, let them hear your voice and you theirs, and it may help to smooth things over," Denny said.

"I am ashamed. They should have been first in my mind." Sarina squared her shoulders. "Yes, you are right. Letters will take a long time, and there is much to explain and much for which to beg their forgiveness. I will call them."

A look of panic filled her eyes. "I need a little time to prepare what I will say to them. I must tell them about being baptized. My mother is open to all religions, to all people.

It is my father who prefers those who have his values and beliefs." She clasped her hands. "Why must there be so many different religions, so many different names for God?"

"Sarina, I know there are many differences and names for God, but the belief in a divinity, in someone or something greater than we are, is a universal belief. In all places, among all peoples, there is a belief that there is someone they can turn to for help and protection. Sometimes life is too big and too complicated for us to cope with alone, and we need someone or something larger than ourselves to turn to."

Sarina nodded. "Hindus are tolerant of other people's ways of worship and do not persecute those whose gods are different from ours, nor do they seek to convert anyone."

"I respect them for that," Denny said. "So, let us go to my cottage and you can call your parents."

She looked at him, shades of emotion crossing her face: panic, then thoughtfulness, followed by resignation. "Yes. Let me do it now, and get it behind me."

Hand in hand they walked to the cottage, and Denny dialed the number that Sarina gave to him and handed her the phone. "It's ringing." Wanting to give her privacy, Denny gestured toward the kitchen, and Sarina nodded.

Far away, yet clear and crisp, her mother was saying hello and expressing her delight on hearing her daughter's voice.

After the amenities—that her sisters and their husbands and children were well, that her father and brother, her aunts and cousins were well, and assurances that she and Sarah were in the best of health and happy—Sarina swallowed hard. Then, speaking calmly, she confessed to her mother the truth about her husband.

"From the moment we boarded the plane, he changed," Sarina said, tears welling in her eyes. "I was in a strange land with people I did not know and customs I did not understand. Zachary abandoned me to play the cards, to gamble away what little money we had. Without the love and compassion of Hannah, and her friends Grace and Amelia, and of course Max, Zachary's father, I do not know how I would have survived. They cared for me. Hannah and Max were there when Sarah was born. She is so beautiful. How you would love to be with her, and she would adore you."

Had she not been seated, Sarina would have collapsed, so weak were her knees. But her mother listened as she told of Zachary's treatment of Max, his rudeness and ungratefulness and how, when he could not have his way, he packed a bag and vanished. Her stomach churning, Sarina explained about Zachary's letter and that she was about to be divorced.

"He sent me a letter saying he will never return, that he does not want a wife and child, a home with me or with anyone. He told me to divorce him." She paused, waiting for her mother's reaction, hoping that she would not reject her, berate her, blame her for not being a good enough wife to Zachary. Then Sarina realized that her mother was sobbing softly, and Sarina began to cry.

Hearing this, Denny came from the kitchen with a damp hand towel, which Sarina pressed to her face. As she listened to her mother's anguish, she realized that this was an inauspicious time to announce that she had fallen in love and wished to marry. They would need many days, even weeks, to consider all the things that had happened to her.

Far away in India, Sarina's mother could barely talk, and she wept for her daughter. Finally, gaining a measure of control, she said, "You should have told us. We would have come and brought you home."

Home to what? To disgrace, to shame? Sarina apologized, then begged forgiveness. "I wanted to show you how strong I was, that I could handle things myself." Her eyes sought Denny's, and the love on his face gave her heart.

"Mama, remember how you say there is always something good to balance the bad? I have good news, as well." She sat straighter, and her voice grew firm and strong. *I am not a little girl lost,* Sarina thought. *I am a woman with a child. I am not begging permission but informing my parents*

*in the nicest way possible, that I have found someone kind
and gentle who loves me and loves Sarah.*

"Mama, it is nearly two years since Zachary is gone. I
will be divorced in a few weeks. I have met a wonderful
man, kind and gentle, who lives in Covington. He is a good
friend of Max and Hannah and highly respected by them.
He wishes to ask you and Papa for my hand in marriage."

She was silent as she listened to her mother's reply.
Then Sarina said, "Yes, I love him, Mama, and yes, he
loves me very much, and he loves Sarah very much and
she loves him. When she sees him, she runs to him with
her arms wide open."

Silence, then. "I am truly sorry not to have told you
before. I wanted to spare you pain. Yes, it was a mistake. I
should have called you immediately." Tears filled her eyes
again.

Denny could hear the irate voice, the weeping, then the
faraway voice on the phone grew calmer and lower until he
could no longer make out Sarina's mother's words.

Sarina looked at Denny, smiled, and nodded. The crisis was over. Her mother was again the practical, realistic
woman she was. But what about Sarina's father?

Sarina nodded, hung up the phone, turned to Denny,
and threw her arms about him. "It will be all right. It is
natural they will have concerns and questions. We have

made a plan. My mother will talk to my father, and when he is calm, they will call me and I will talk to him. After that, you will phone and talk with him several times, so that he feels he has a sense of who you are. Then you will ask for my hand in marriage."

"Did you tell her I'm a Christian pastor?" Denny asked, knowing she had not.

Taking his hand, Sarina led him to the small living room. "I will tell her when we speak again. Her experience of American men of God has been Catholic missionaries who do not marry. I will explain that there are other denominations with pastors who marry and have families. She will discuss this with my brother, and Sanjay will find a book about it to show to my father. If it is written, my father will accept it better. Mama cares only if you are a good man who will treat me with kindness and take care of me."

"You did not tell her you had Sarah baptized."

"No. It was too much to tell all at one moment. Next time I will tell her. I will tell her also that I will stay in America, married or not, for the opportunities for myself and for my daughter. She will accept that I have changed, that I am a grown woman, more easily than my father. He would keep me a little girl forever if he could." Sarina tilted her chin with pride and her eyes brightened. "She will come to our wedding, even if my father will not. And she will bring one or more of my sisters. Amala perhaps, or Pari."

Denny looked at her, and she could see his love shining in his eyes. "I love you so much. I know how hard it was for you. I'm proud of you."

"Mama will come," Sarina repeated happily. "It will be good." She held her hands out in front of her. "She will paint my hands with henna."

When her mother called a few days later, she told Sarina that she had explained it all to her father and calmed his ravings. Ten days later she phoned again for an arranged conference call to introduce them to Denny.

"There must be several talks before your Denny asks your papa," Sarina's mother had explained.

The booming voice of Sarina's father, Ravi, clearly defined his role as patriarch of his family and a man not to be trifled with. Denny had no intention of trifling. He listened politely and, having been coached by Sarina, expressed his regret that he was unable to come to India to meet the family. Sarina had sent pictures. The father said he imagined Denny as taller and wearing long robes like the missionary priests he had known. They spoke for a half hour, Denny listening and responding in turn.

After several weeks and many conversations, Sarina's father said, "I have had my son Sanjay check you out." He chuckled. "Like in your American spy movies, and I am satisfied that you are a good man. Now you may ask me for my daughter's hand in marriage."

Denny breathed a sigh of relief, lifted his eyes to heaven, and offered a silent *Thank you, God*. Then he formally requested permission to marry Sarina, and permission was formally granted.

"I have consulted the astrologer," Ravi said in his booming voice. "Next July is the best time for you to marry. If all goes well we will come with the whole family, and we will make a wedding you will remember." The phone went dead then, leaving Denny weak-kneed but happy that this ordeal was behind him.

"It is done," Denny told Max, whom he had kept informed as things went along. "But Ravi has declared that we cannot be married until next July. Some astrologer says so."

"I know you're eager to be married, but it's probably a good thing to have this time, and I would honor Ravi's belief system," Max said. "July's a fine month. Sarina will have time to adjust to being a Christian, and people will have time to get used to her as a Christian."

"I'll make the best of it, Max," Denny said, smiling. "Thanks for your wise counsel."

22

Ancestors in Walhalla

THE DRIVE DOWN THE mountain to Walhalla in western South Carolina was pleasant. Along the way, Grace exclaimed at the new upscale housing developments on both sides of the road. As she and Bob crossed a branch of Lake Keowee just below the dam at Lake Jocassee, they were amazed at the number of homes set back among groves of trees and boat docks dotting the lakefront.

Grace's son, Roger Singleton, an engineer turned horticulturist, had moved to South Carolina several years earlier and bought a tract of land along a river in the small community of Salem. There, he had established a tree nursery from which he supplied flowering trees to local nurseries.

Grace looked forward to seeing her son and hearing about his growing business, and most especially learning what he had unearthed about Thomas Mueller's ancestors.

WHEN THEY HAD CALLED him, Roger found the whole idea of reuniting families fascinating. Immediately after Bob's first call he had spent several days at the Walhalla courthouse poring over old documents, and had been successful in his search. "Wait and see," he had said when his mother pressed him on the phone. "Wait and see."

"I hate it when Roger's secretive. He could have told me what he found," Grace said as they turned from Highway 11 onto the road leading to Roger's property.

"It's not long now, and soon you'll know everything," Bob assured her.

"What do you think? Is it good news or bad news?"

"I think it's good news. Now relax and enjoy the ride."

"Then why wouldn't Roger just come right out and tell us?" Grace persisted.

"Grace, honey, you're worrying for nothing. We'll be there in ten minutes."

Grace rested her head against the seat and closed her eyes as the pleasant pastoral countryside slipped past them. She had been here many times and could see in her mind's eye the falling-down farmhouse, now fully restored by caring new owners to its original grace and charm, and the small man-made lake and half dozen homes clustered around it.

When Bob turned into the driveway of Roger's wood and glass home, he said, "I really like Roger's place. He did a great job designing his house."

"I like it, too," Grace replied, smoothing her hair. "I especially enjoy sitting on his front porch, looking down on the field and the river." She released her seat belt and reached for her purse on the floor by her feet. "Remember when Roger first moved here, how the banks of the river were so overgrown you couldn't see the water?"

"He's cleaned away the bushes and opened the view," Bob said. "This whole area is lovely, although it's not as dramatic as the high mountains where we live. It's pleasant and relaxing. I enjoy coming down here."

Before Bob could open his car door, Roger stepped from the house and came to greet them. Grace and Roger hugged, and he hugged Bob as well. "Good to see you both.

Come on inside. I made a salad for lunch, then we can go over what I've unearthed about your Tom Mueller."

Grace hated to take time for lunch. "Tell us what you found first, then we'll eat."

"Relax," Bob said as Roger led them into the house. "Roger will share all the information he has in a few minutes."

She wished Bob would stop telling her to relax. How could she relax? She *had* to know, and soon.

They stepped into the large open room that housed the kitchen, dining, and living areas.

"Okay, come look at this," Roger said, bending to Grace's desire. On the dining room table he had spread a large sheet of paper, and Grace immediately recognized the circles and lines as a genealogy chart.

Roger pointed to the top row of circles. "Tom Mueller's family was among the first families to settle in this area. There were four Mueller brothers, and I focused on Kurt Mueller's line of descent since he's the important ancestor involved.

"Kurt married Wilhelmina Franklin and they had three kids: Kurt Junior, Marina, and Karla. Tom descended from Kurt Junior and his son, so I didn't follow the other brother's and sisters' lines. I hope that was all right?"

Grace nodded. It seemed so simple looking at the chart, but it wasn't. Thinking of the time involved in putting it all together, she smiled at her son and patted his shoulder. "I appreciate all the work you went to, Roger."

"It was fun, actually. I enjoyed it. They were very helpful at the courthouse."

They turned their attention to the chart, and their eyes followed Roger's finger almost to the bottom of the page. "Here he is: Thomas Alfred Mueller, the great-great-great-grandson of Kurt Mueller, the original German settler in Walhalla." He tapped two circles at the very bottom. "And here are your Tom's living relatives in this area: Ada and Arnold Pennington, and Ben and Louise Mueller. Ben and Ada are brother and sister. The Penningtons live in Clemson. Ada teaches middle school over in Clemson and her husband Arnold's with the agriculture department at the university.

"I intended to call them, introduce myself, and arrange to go over and tell them about you and your box of diaries and letters, but I haven't had a chance." He tapped the other circle. "Ben Mueller owns a construction company. You see his signs everywhere. I am sorry, but I didn't call him, either."

"Not to worry, Roger. We can do it, can't we, Bob?" Grace nudged Bob's arm. "We can stay over with Roger a night or two and make contact with these people. That's all right with you, isn't it, Roger?"

Roger smiled at his mother and nodded. "Sure. You're welcome to stay as long as you'd like. I'm in and out so I can't guarantee you home-cooked meals."

"I'll take care of the meals," Grace said.

Bob rubbed his chin and looked thoughtful. "I'll call Martin and cancel our golf game tomorrow. There's something else I had on my calendar for Monday. What was it? Oh, yes, a dental appointment for a cleaning. I'll reschedule that, too." He looked at Grace. "What do you want to do about a change of clothes and something to sleep in? We could drive into Seneca to Kmart and pick up a few things, maybe have dinner over that way?"

Grace slipped her arm through her son's and looked up at him. He was a head taller than she was, and when she looked into his eyes, she saw his father, Ted, who had passed away many years ago. "You'll come with us, Roger?"

"Sure. I'll drive. You must be tired of driving, Bob."

"I'd appreciate that, Roger," Bob replied.

They ate lunch then, sitting out on the covered front porch overlooking the river. The day was partly cloudy, the sun emerging from between fast-moving gray clouds and vanishing as quickly. When the sun disappeared, a pleasant breeze wafted up from the river.

Grace smiled. Something in the air, some unidentified

smell, reminded her of her childhood, of a quick-flowing river and fishing with her father. There had been a wild vine in bloom, and her father had picked a blossom and handed it to her. She had treasured that yellow flower and pressed it in a book, which unfortunately had been lost in the fire that swept away the original farmhouse they'd lived in in Covington several years ago. For the life of her, now, she couldn't bring to mind the name of that vine, although she and her father had looked it up in a book he'd gotten from the library.

In the far distance the mountains of North Carolina assumed that bluish haze that lent them their name, the Blue Ridge Mountains. *Today,* Grace thought, *is one of those lovely days in which I'm glad to be alive.*

"The river's running high today," Roger said. "We've had an abundance of rain this summer. It's been great for the new trees, gave them a good start." He and Bob chatted then about the business, how sales had been this past summer, and about Roger's plans for the future. "I've contracted to have a greenhouse built over there." Roger pointed to the far right of the field below them. "There's a growing market for fresh, organic vegetables year round."

"Right you are," Bob replied. "This year we all got together and put in a garden. We've had lots of fresh veggies."

Grace nodded. "Gardening's a lot of work at our age. If Hannah hadn't had raised beds put in our backyard, I wouldn't have been able to get in there and weed."

Bob changed the subject. "Do you do any home landscaping, Roger?"

Roger shook his head. "Nope. Too much chasing here, there, and everywhere. I just grow them and deliver my specialty trees to nurseries."

He looks content, Grace thought. *For so many years, he was so restless. I believe he hated being an engineer. Once, he told me that he had gone into that career because he thought it would please his father. Fathers and sons—how hard that relationship is. Roger never felt truly loved by Ted. But this isn't a day for remembering sad things. It's good to be here, to see my son happy with his work and his life, to spend time with him in his lovely home.*

Roger caught her eye. "You look tired. Do you want to rest a while, Mom, or shall we go?"

Grace raised her arms above her head and stretched her back and shoulders. "I admit, I'm tired, but if I lie down, I'll not be able to push myself out of the door later. Let's go and get it over with. When we come back, I'll have a shower and sleep."

Later that afternoon, after shopping and picking up barbecued chicken for dinner, after Grace and Bob had showered and changed into comfortable pajamas and robes, they once again sat and relaxed on the porch. Roger handed Grace his phone. "I think this would be a good time to call the Muellers and the Penningtons, Mom."

Grace cradled the phone in her hands. "What shall I say to them?" She looked at Bob. "Maybe it would be better to write them?"

"We're here, honey. That's what we came for, remember? Just dial one of those numbers, introduce yourself, and tell them about the box and the letters. Tell them we're here for a day or two, and could we meet for a cup of coffee?"

"You make it sound so simple." She set the phone on her lap and brought her hands to her chest. "My heart's racing."

"Now, Gracie, girl." Bob reached over and put an arm about her shoulders. "This isn't like you're calling to say someone died. Who isn't interested in their ancestors? Come on now, let me dial for you. Which family would you prefer that I call first?"

Grace was silent for a time, "The Penningtons, I think. I'll do it." The number rang many times, and just as Grace was about to hang up, a child's voice said, "My mama's in the bathroom. Who is it?"

Braced for an adult, Grace was taken aback. Then she

sat up straight and said, "My name is Grace. Please tell your mama I will call back in fifteen minutes."

"Okay," the child replied and hung up.

"That child sounded about four years old. I wonder if her mother will ever get that message," Grace said. "Let's try the Muellers."

A man picked up on the first ring, and Grace wondered if he had been preparing to make a call.

"Hello," she said. "My name is Grace Singleton and—" Grace looked startled and set the phone in her lap. "He hung up—just like that."

"Maybe whoever answered thought you were a salesperson. Haven't you ever just hung up on them?" Roger asked.

"Why, yes, I have. So, what am I to do?" Grace looked from Bob to Roger to Bob.

"Just start with, 'I am not selling anything,'" Roger suggested.

Grace shoved his phone at him. "I can't do this."

"Here, let me." Bob took the phone, dialed the number, and waited. On the third ring, the phone was answered by a man. "Hello, this is not a sales call," Bob hastened to assure him.

"What is it, then?" the man asked.

"It's about an ancestor of yours who went off to fight in the Civil War and never came back."

"And what, you're making a claim to his estate?"

"Goodness, no. A tin box was unearthed by a bulldozer on our land in North Carolina. Inside were diaries and packets of letters written by a Tom Mueller from Walhalla. He was wounded badly and left to die in a trench after a battle. An old woman found him, took him to North Carolina where she lived, and nursed him back to health. We're trying to find his descendants. We'd like to give them copies of the letters and diaries."

The man on the line was silent for so long, Bob was certain he had hung up the phone. Bob was about to do the same when the voice said, "This is Ben Mueller. I'm sorry I was so rude. My wife's had a rash of obscene calls lately. They're supposed to change our number, and there's been a delay. What did you say your name was?"

"Bob Richardson. I'm here with Grace Singleton, whose son lives in Salem. I think you'd find the story interesting. Would it be possible for us to have coffee someplace convenient for you?" He fell silent, but nodded periodically.

Grace shifted in her chair, eager for news of what was taking place.

"The Steak House Cafeteria in Walhalla? Lunch at noon tomorrow. We'll meet you there, and thank you. Yes, of course. Here's the number in Salem where we can be reached." He gave the man Roger's number and hung up. "Ben Mueller was curious and receptive."

"Not to me, he wasn't," Grace said.

"His wife's been getting obscene phone calls, and they were waiting for their phone number to be changed," Bob said.

"Do I sound like a man or an obscene phone caller?" Grace walked away in a huff, and Bob thought it best to drop the matter.

"How about showing me one of those letters," Roger asked.

"They're in my purse, I'll go get them." Grace trotted down the hall to the bedroom and returned with a letter in hand. Settled on the sofa, she began:

> Miss Ella Mae wasn't a woman to talk much, but one day she told Tom and me that many mountain women she knew had visions—they knew what was about to happen or had happened. She said it was a vision that had taken her down to that field that day to hunt her grandson.
>
> "Sittin' right in this rocker, I was, on this here porch," she said. "Sun was a-settin' over yonder mountain, and

I seen his face clear and I heard his voice a-callin' me to come git him. So I hitched old Sam to the wagon, got me a jug of water and another of strong corn liquor, a pan of cornbread, quilts for sleepin', and started down the mountain. I was a ways back in the hills when I heard the guns and the screamin' comin' from the valley. I seen smoke and smelled gunpowder. 'Twasn't nothing I could do 'septin to sit in that old wagon and pray 'til it was done and quiet.

"I found my boy gone from this world. He was callin' me from that porch to bury him, else he woulda lay for the wolves and buzzards to git him. I'd brung me a shovel, so I dug me a hole. Took all afternoon 'til I finished, and I buried him, and told the Lord he was baptized and prayed the Lord to keep his soul."

"I'm sorry you lost him," I said.

She shrugged. "Life's about givin' and takin', havin' and losin'."

We sat silent. The sunset turned gold, lavender, and gray, and we lit a lantern, for we were shelling beans. After a time, I asked Miss Ella Mae, "Do you have visions often?"

"All my born days, I been seein' things gonna happen. I know'd I was gonna marry up with Wayne Evans

when I done hear his voice in the yard. He done come to buy a pig off Pa, and I seen when Ma was gonna die. After Junior come, I prayed for more children to help in the fields, 'til I seen I weren't gonna have no more, and I stopped prayin' and told Big Wayne, and he cried. I never seen him cry afore or after."

She stopped for a moment, snapped a bean hard, then took a handkerchief from her pocket and dabbed her eyes. Tom and I kept on snapping beans, thinking she was finished telling.

But she continued, "I know'd my son, Wayne Junior, was taken by the water afore those men brung the news." Miss Ella Mae looked shy then, and a blush came on her face, and she looked at me and at Tom. "When I seen you two layin' in that ditch, I heard a voice say, 'Carry 'em home, Ella Mae,' an I seen you was gonna heal up from your wounds and you was gonna be like sons to me. And you is just that."

That was the end of the telling, but it left me wondering about fate and predestination and my life, and wondering what my future might be and if Miss Ella Mae could see that, and if she did, would she tell me?

I was lonely at first, up on that mountain, especially as we couldn't go to the village and meet other folks except for Miss Maggie and Issy for nearly a year, until the war ended.

I thought a lot, then, of home, about how Ma, Pa, and I used to sit out on our front porch in town, and people would stroll by and wave or stop to chat. Miss Ella Mae figured I needed to keep busy, not to think about home or the things I'd seen at war, and she must have talked to Tom about it.

Because the next thing I knew, Tom was showing me how to hitch the plow and walk behind old Sam. I wasn't much good at it, at first. Old Sam had a mind of his own, and many a day he dragged me, rather than me controlling him. I can't count the times I fell behind that plow, once right down on my face, getting a mouthful of dirt and bruises on my chin and hands. I cussed more then than I ever did in all my life.

I was sure I'd never make a farmer, but you should see me now. I can walk behind that horse and plow furrows in a straight line. Old Sam doesn't try any nonsense on me anymore, and I can plant seed, hoe, weed, and cultivate the earth. Growing food, seeing ears of corn ripen, and picking beans and tomatoes has become a pleasure in my life. I wonder sometimes if Miss Ella Mae saw that I would make a farmer, and a good one, too? She never would say, although I pressed her once.

Roger shook himself as if to bring himself back to this time and place. "Like me, John changed his whole life. He came to love the earth as I do." He grinned and held out his hand to Grace. "I wonder if *this* was all meant to be, my being here. Let's walk in the garden by the river, Mom." He turned to Bob. "Want to join us?"

Bob shook his head. "I'll watch the ball game."

Grace took her son's arm and they left the house. "You're happy here, aren't you?" she asked as they walked along the paved path Roger had had constructed alongside the river. Here and there he had placed a cedar bench, and they sat on one and watched Little River purr past, bearing twigs and leaves to some destination hidden by a bend in the river.

"I certainly am. Best thing I ever did was buy this land, go to the university, and change my profession."

"It makes me so happy to see you settled and happy."

"I love this land, my work, my life, and I have friends in the area now. The nicest couple moved in a mile up the main road. Their kids come over and help me weed. It's a good life."

"It's a real pleasure to be here with you."

He turned to her. "Mom. Don't worry about these people, how they receive you. You're doing the right thing, to find them and bring their relatives to their attention. Once they get over the shock, they can't help but be interested in what you have to say and to show them." Roger squeezed her hand gently. "It'll turn out just fine."

She squeezed his hand back, and they sat in silence in the gathering dusk, happy simply to be together in this place, at this time.

23

Ben and Louise Mueller

TALL AND LANKY, HIS hands big and bony, Ben Mueller appeared nervous. His wife, Louise, short with inquisitive blue eyes and light brown hair pinned back in a bun at the nape of her neck, seemed calm as they stepped from their car and walked toward the threesome sitting on the iron bench in front of The Steak House Cafeteria.

Grace, Bob, and Roger stood. Introductions were made and hands shaken.

"We're sorry we're late," Ben said. "One of the kids fell, and his mother here had to stop to fix him." He looked at Grace. "You know how that is."

Grace smiled. "I surely do. We're so glad to meet you."

Introductions completed, they went inside, and Grace greeted the owner, Abed, whom they had come to know on their visits to Roger. They stood in a short line for their food, which was served cafeteria style. Grace, Bob, and Roger chose fried chicken, for which The Steak House was famous.

As always, at noon the restaurant was crowded. Brisk conversation and laughter rose from the main dining room, and they took a table at one end of the new dining room. Once seated, Grace explained how they had come into possession of the box. As she spoke of the letters and diaries, her eyes lit up and her voice grew animated.

"I've brought along several of his letters for you to read. There are many more, of course, and four diaries."

"So, you're telling me that one of my ancestors joined up to fight in the Civil War, survived the carnage of that war, and chose never to come home?" Ben's voice was laced with disbelief. He shook his head. "Can't say I want to know anything about this man. Why in heaven's name would he stay up there in North Carolina and not tell his people he was alive?"

"Why didn't he come home?" Louise asked in a gentler voice.

Grace stressed the serious nature of Tom's wounds,

and that without Miss Ella Mae Evans's help, he could never have survived. "Ella Mae Evans was poor and old, and all alone in the world. She had lost her only son in an accident years earlier and her daughter-in-law had died in childbirth. Her only grandson had been killed on that battlefield where she found Tom and John. She saved their lives, and I think that a deep sense of gratitude and loyalty colored their decisions to stay with Ella Mae.

"Tom also wrote that his mother died when he was very young and he did not like his father's new wife, also that there were many younger than himself to help with the farm. I've lain awake at night trying to fathom what it was like for them—what they thought, why they made the choices they did—but who can enter the mind of anyone else? Especially someone who lived so many years ago and under such different circumstances?" Grace reached for her glass of iced tea.

Louise nodded. "I quite understand. I can't fathom what's going on in the minds of my own children, or even Ben, here, sometimes." She smiled at her husband and patted his hand. He smiled at her.

"Okay, I hear what you're saying," Ben said, "but why are you wanting to tell me about this Tom or show me his letters?"

"Because we thought—the ladies I share a home with in Covington, Hannah and Amelia—we thought that if we could trace Tom's family of origin, we could invite the Mueller descendants who live here, and the Evans descendants who live in Black Mountain, to come to Covington at Christmastime, have a celebration, introduce you to one another, and give each family copies of his ancestor's letters and diaries."

Ben looked grim. He set down his fork and shoved his chair back from the table. Grace expected him to stand and walk away, but he crossed his long legs and looked at Louise, who nodded at him and patted his arm. "Now honey, since we're here, why not at least take a look at those letters?"

Grace reached into her purse and handed Ben several letters she had tied with a thin green ribbon. "His writing isn't always easy to read. If you have trouble, I've read them so many times, I've pretty much figured out the words."

Ben held the small package of letters as if it were a delicate piece of crystal. Finally Louise took it from him, untied the ribbon, and laid the four letters in a row in front of them. "Is there an order in which we should read them?" she asked Grace.

Grace leaned across the table. "They don't all have

dates, but they were one atop the other when we found them, and we marked them to keep some kind of order, if that had been intended. See the mark in the upper right corner, small numbers in pencil?" She changed the place of two of the letters. "They're in order now, left to right."

Louise carefully picked up the first letter, slid it from its envelope, and unfolded the crinkled paper.

We was eatin' mostly hardtack and salt pork by then.

Louise paused. "What's hardtack?"

"A flour and water biscuit about a half-inch thick. I looked it up. I didn't know what it was, either."

Louise turned her attention back to the letter:

> *Times was that hardtack was so hard, ain't no one couldda eat it without they broke it to pieces and soften it in water or gin, whatever we got, and you got to be careful it ain't get gummy. Coffee done taste like mud, and we was sleepin' in tents fit for dogs.*

I seen men and no more'n boys die. Bill Bridges was workin' the ox team that was pullin' a supply wagon when he took it in the back. There weren't no doctors where we was to tend him, and we buried him in a hole we dug in that there mud. The captain said for me to take Bill's place. Guess I was the first his eyes done fell on. Thinkin' back, he needed them wagons more than he needed a grunt like me, but I sure hated crackin' a whip keepin' them stupid ox movin'. I got me outta that job soon's I could figure a way.

Ben's voice was disdainful when he interrupted his wife. "Tom wasn't very well educated, was he?"

"No, he wasn't." Grace felt protective of Tom. "He was just a young farm boy, but he brought his farming skills with him, and it was Tom who kept them all alive that first winter. You need to read the diaries and all his letters to get a sense of who he was—honest and hardworking, kind, a good man. In the war he managed to learn a lot about being a medic, which really helped him later. He wasn't stupid by any means, just not educated, though he certainly was able to write." Grace looked deep into Ben Mueller's eyes. "There had to be something special about him, that he rose above the normal hate of an enemy soldier lying there in the ditch beside him. Without Tom and his medical skills, John would have bled to death. Those two soldiers became as close as brothers."

Grace caught Bob's eye, which cautioned her to calm down, to take it easy, not to push this man. *It's a shock for him, hearing about Tom Mueller,* she thought, and she fell silent.

"A medic, you say? One day he's driving oxen and then he's a medic?" Ben guffawed.

"I chose these letters because they explain how that happened," Grace said. She wanted to snatch up the letters and leave.

Bob gently pressed his knee against hers under the table as if to say, *Whoa there, Gracie girl, we're here. Let's see this through.*

"It sounds horrible, what the poor fellow had to go through," Louise said. She looked at Grace. "Our nephew's over in Iraq. We're all so anxious and upset. We begged him not to enlist, but the recruiting officer bribed him—you couldn't call it anything else—with a big chunk of cash. That's all these kids can see, dollars, and they think they're invincible." Her eyes filled with tears.

"I am so sorry," Grace said.

Louise shivered as if shaking away the memory, and turned her attention back to the letter:

❧❧

*Early on, afore we joined us up with the Army
of the Conferderacy at Chattanooga and the fightin'
got goin', and afore my friend from home, Eden, got
hisself killed, and a new friend, Joe, deserted, we'd
kick back and talk 'bout home, 'bout farmin'. That
old red clay we'd hated did sure seem like heaven
then. One time I heard a captain sayin' how it was
sure hard to fight them Yanks in these here mountains,
how you ain't know what's a-comin' round a bend or
'cross a mountain. Next day they beat us back, them
Yanks.*

"I wonder who they were, Eden and Joe?" Ben remarked, and Louise shushed him with a finger to her lips.

*Some of 'em fellows was real disgustin'. They never
washed none, and they stunk bad. Other fellows
washed their clothes in the kettles our food was
cooked in. I done wash my clothes when they was
stiff and smellin' bad and we come to a creek or a
river.*

Louise put down the letter again and looked intently at Grace. "It sounds to me that perhaps these letters took the place of therapy. They provided a catharsis for Tom, and probably helped him get past the horror of what he'd been through." She tapped the page with her finger. "This letter, and probably the others, were never meant to be mailed to anyone. You say the other fellow also wrote and never mailed his letters?"

Grace nodded.

"Somehow, these two young soldiers figured out that it helped them to write about it."

Ben shifted in his chair, leaned forward, and slipped his arm about his wife's shoulders. "Louise here's a counselor up at the community college. She's helped a lot of people, and not just students. I built her a real nice office in our house, private entrance and all. Lots of folks come to talk to her."

Grace stared at Louise in amazement. "Thank you. You've answered the question of why they never sent the letters home. How stupid of me not to have realized their true intent." Grace turned to Bob. "I can't wait to get home and tell Hannah and Amelia!"

Louise had picked up another of the letters, opened it, and read it silently. Then she turned to her husband. "Just listen to this, Ben. Tom may not write well, but see how cleverly he worked his way to become a medic."

Ain't had 'nough ambulance corpsmen, and too many wounded. We foot soldiers done carried most of the wounded to the medics. I carried a heck of a lotta men off the field. I seen ambulance corpsmen wearin' green bands they called a chevron, so I stealed me the cap and band off a corpsman layin' dead, and they figured me for bein' a medic. Next thing, I'm keepin' the box hung under the ambulance driver's seat full of supplies.

I ain't never gonna forget how many boxes I packed up with bed sacks, cans of beef stock, leather buckets, camp kettles, a lantern and a candle, tin plates, tin tumblers, and afore a battle, ten pounds of hardtack.

One day, I'm passin' the ambulance wagon, and I hear a man beggin' 'em not to cut off his arm. I look inside, and the doc sees my cap and calls me to hand him the cloth with the fumes to put the fellow to sleep. Lucky I ain't fainted when the doc sawed off the fellow's arm six inches under his shoulder and threw it in a pile of parts—feet, legs, arms—in a corner. I near to puked.

Doc, he says for me to stay with the fellow, so I sit aside him 'til he done wakes up. His eyes, they gone wide when he seen a stump where his arm supposen to be, and he let out a scream and fainted dead away. I done thought he was dead. He weren't no more than a boy, sixteen maybe. Turns out, he weren't dead, and they mustta sent him off somewhere 'cause I never did lay eyes on him again.

"See, Ben." Louise nudged her husband's arm. "Grace is right. Just because Tom hadn't learned to write properly, it doesn't mean he wasn't smart. We may not know what he went on to do with his life, but I think he was quite intelligent."

"We do know something about his life," Grace said. "Milo Evans, a relative of John Foster, is into genealogy, and he did a chart for Tom. He became a farmer, owned his own land, and raised cows for milking and beef. He married a woman named Glory, who had three small children, and he had several children of his own. Everything we read about Tom indicated he was kind, caring, and thoughtful. He and Glory took Miss Ella Mae to live with them and cared for her until she died."

"You're really involved with these men, aren't you?" Ben said.

"I guess I am. We all are, Amelia and Hannah and I. And Milo located a family member of yours through the genealogy chart on Tom. His name's Matthew Evans, and he's a professor of literature at Warren Wilson College in Swannanoa, near Asheville."

"A professor? How lovely," Louise said. "Does he have a family?"

"Yes, a wife and two sons," Grace replied.

"What am I supposed to do, rush up there and hug him? Hell no—I'm not doing anything of the kind," Ben said.

"Ben." Louise turned to him. "He may be your relative, and maybe he's a very nice person. Why wouldn't we at least meet him, have lunch, perhaps? We could make a day of it." She looked at Bob. "How long a drive is it to Asheville?"

"About two and a half hours from Walhalla to Covington."

"Ada, Ben's sister, might want to go along." She looked at Ben. "This Matthew is her relative, too. We must show Ada and Arnold the letters. It's exciting, Ben. If it were my relative that I didn't know about, I'd be eager to meet him. In fact, I am eager to meet this professor and his family, and Milo, who knows so much about genealogy." Louise turned to Grace. "May we keep these letters for a few days to show to my sister-in-law, Ada, and her husband, Arnold?"

Grace looked at Bob, who said, "We're not in a position to leave the letters with you, but if you'd like, we could meet you back here tomorrow and bring the letters and the diary we brought."

Grace said, "You're also welcome to come to my place in Salem this evening, or tomorrow with your family. You can take your time, sit, relax, and read them."

Louise said, "I'd like to read the other two letters now, and we'll talk to Ada and set up a date." She picked up the third letter and began:

We done march or fight all day and when the food was scarce, we foraged for food at night, goin' into sheep pens stealin' sheep an hopin' to get off before the noise brung the owner out with his shotgun, or raidin' a henhouse. After a time, folks begun keepin' hens and such inside their houses, so they was hard to get.

Was an unlucky man livin' next the marchin' rout. Officers mainly, 'cause it was easy, marchin' in and outta them fine houses, takin' what they pleased. After a time, people was laid bare of goods and livestock and stopped plantin' their fields. They took to hidin' what they had, especially after Rebs and Yanks done tramped back and forth, losin' a piece of ground, gainin' it back, losin' it again, leavin' local folks hardly nothin' to hide.

We stole every horse come upon. Once we'd used up its strength and the poor creature's bones stuck out and it couldn't bare to stand on its legs, it was left behind for some farmer to find and tend, to be stole again 'til the poor beast fell dead where he was a-standin'. Now mules, they was a different story. Ain't nobody work a mule to death. They was the workhorse of the army, ours and theirs.

I seen war turn good men bad, with more sins to pray God to forgive than if they'd lived a lifetime. I seen men walk into houses and bayonet mirrors, smash piano keys, and pitch crockery outtin windows just for the seemin' joy of it. Lord knows I done my share of raidin', for times food was scarce. I stole from curing houses early on in the war, and cattle, too, but I swear on Ma's grave, I ain't never pillage no inside property.

Louise's face had grown increasingly flushed as she read and she stopped, folded the letter and slipped it into its envelope, then tied all four letters with the green ribbon. "That's about all I can deal with just now." She handed them to Grace.

"Some of the letters *are* hard to read," Grace said. "Not many, though. Most reveal character and speak of their lives with Miss Ella Mae, not of the war."

Grace regretted including that letter. It had been difficult for her to read and for Amelia especially. She couldn't tear it up, though; it wasn't hers to destroy.

"We'll call Ada as soon as we get home," Louise said. "I know she'll want to see the letters, and then I'll be ready to read the fourth letter." She turned in her chair to face her husband. Her voice was calm and firm, her feelings, whatever they might be, well under control. "We can drive out to Salem tomorrow after church, right, Ben?"

After a moment, Ben nodded. "Why not? And we'll bring Ada. She's entitled to a say in all of this."

BLOND AND BLUE-EYED, WITH ruddy complexions, Ada and Arnold looked like brother and sister, with Ada being the more affable and outgoing. Louise had explained it all, and Ada read the letters with great interest, appearing not be put off by some of the details, as her sister-in-law had been.

"I want to meet Professor Matthew Evans and his family." She set a letter down and turned to Arnold. "We'll drive up there with Louise and Ben."

Arnold nodded. "Sure, if you want to."

"I want to." Ada addressed her brother. "When can you get away, Ben?"

"Some Sunday, maybe."

"Next Sunday," Ada declared. "I know you, Ben. If we don't pin you down, you'll find an excuse to work on Sunday."

"We have to phone these people and introduce ourselves, and see what day suits them," Louise said.

"I'll call Matthew Evans and set it up," Ada said.

Louise looked at Grace, sitting quietly on the other side of Roger's living room. "What do you think, Grace? Will Matthew Evans be amenable to hearing from us?"

"He was fascinated by the letters and diaries. He came to our place in Covington, and when he read them, his enthusiasm grew. I think he'd be happy to hear from you. He mentioned he'd been planning for years to come down to Lake Jocassee for fishing and never did."

Arnold slapped his knee. "Well, we'll invite him on down, and we'll take him and his family out on the *Anna*

Marie." He looked at Grace and Bob. "That's our boat, named for our daughters, Anna and Marie."

They rose then, thanked Grace and Bob, and wished them a safe ride back up the mountain.

Grace hugged and thanked Roger for making it so easy for them to be in touch with the Walhalla relatives; then she and Bob drove home, satisfied at the outcome of their visit.

24

News from Amelia

"DO YOU THINK MILO found what he wanted to and they're on their way home?" Grace asked Hannah over breakfast.

Hannah took a long drink of water. "They've been gone long enough, but we have no idea what they've accomplished." She shoved her chair back and stood. "You could call Amelia again. You have her number?"

Grace nodded. "I haven't wanted to bother them."

"Go ahead and give her a call. If she's not there, leave a message and she'll call back. If they've checked out, the innkeepers will tell you."

"Maybe I should wait to hear from her," Grace said.

"If it's going to worry you, call her, Grace."

Grace looked thoughtful. "Maybe I will."

The desk clerk rang Amelia's room, and she answered on the first ring. "Forgive me, Grace, we should have called, but we haven't stopped for a minute. You can't believe all that Milo's found out! He's been able to fill in John Foster's genealogy chart and he's located relatives—a Great-Uncle Henry something and his family. I've heard so many names lately, I can't keep them straight. People here have been incredibly cooperative. Milo's in heaven."

"And you're having a good time?"

"This is a delightful town. Folks are very friendly."

"I'm eager to hear about John's ancestors."

Amelia's voice fell to almost a whisper. "One of John's ancestors was jailed for making counterfeit money back in the seventeen hundreds." Her voice returned to normal. "Most of his ancestors were farmers, although one of them was a well-respected furniture maker.

"John's mother was a schoolteacher, and the town has restored the schoolhouse she taught in. It's a stark log room with a stove in the middle and a sloping shelf built all around the wall. Older children sat on backless benches facing that shelf. The littlest kids sat on benches with no backs in the center of the room around the stove. When the teacher wanted to talk to one of the children sitting on the bench facing the wall, the child had to swing his or her legs over the bench to face the schoolmarm. Can you imagine learning anything in a situation like that? Oh, and John's father kept books at a button factory. At one time there were several hatmaking and button industries in Newtown.

"We also learned that John's family lived within the town limits, and that he had two sisters and a brother. Milo was fortunate to find a copybook in his sister's handwriting. It was in the historical society's collection."

"Amazing."

"When he told me about it, he cried," Amelia said. "To be able to read words written in John Foster's sister's own hand. That was amazing." She was silent a moment. "His sister, Flora, thought that her brother joined the Union Army because he had a wild nature and couldn't settle down to a stable life."

"If I recall, John wrote something about joining to save the Union in one of the diaries, but then he thought maybe he'd used that excuse to get away from Emily and responsibilities. His sister wasn't far off the mark," Grace said.

"And Grace, just as we thought," Amelia said, "Emily remarried—a shopkeeper named Ernest Burns, and little

Iris became Iris Burns. She married and had children, so John's line went in that direction, as well."

Before Grace could respond, Amelia continued. "Milo's had several meetings with the town historian, Dan Cruson. He's given Milo a lot of time and lots of information. He's written a book called *A Mosaic of Newtown History*. That's where Milo first read about the button and comb factories."

"Button and comb factories?"

"Yes. Buttons made from hide and bone. There was quite a butchering and meatpacking industry in Newtown in the eighteen fifties, and it supplied bone and hide to make combs and buttons. That's where John's father kept books, in a button factory. I said that, didn't I? It must have been so sad for his folks, thinking John died in the war."

Not to be outdone, Grace said, "We were able to locate Tom's descendants, Ben and Louise Mueller and Ada and Arnold Pennington in Walhalla. They're coming here soon to meet Matthew Evans. Louise is a counselor and she said she thought the letters were never meant to be sent home. They were catharsis for the men, a way they could unload their thoughts and feelings about the war and their lives."

"Still, they could have sent one letter after the war to let their people know they were alive and not coming home," Amelia said.

"We'll never know why they chose not to do that," Grace replied.

"You're right, of course. Why do I worry myself about it?" Amelia said.

"Because you're a caring person," Grace replied, then asked, "When are you coming home?"

"Couple of days, I imagine. This afternoon we're going to visit an artist, Patricia Barkman, at her studio on some lake. There are so many lakes around here, I can't keep track."

Grace looked at the kitchen clock. She'd promised to have lunch with Velma in South Asheville at some new restaurant Velma wanted to try. She'd better get off the phone and get going.

"I have to go, Amelia. Let us know when you're coming home."

"I will. See you soon."

25

The Accident

WHEN VELMA SUGGESTED THE new restaurant south of Asheville last evening, Grace, concerned about gas prices and distances, suggested the Athens Restaurant in Weaverville.

"I've got my heart set on this new place. Everyone says the food's fantastic," Velma had replied. "Conserve gas tomorrow."

Velma had also told her that Frank and Alma had had a big to-do that she had heard from her kitchen window, which faced Alma's parlor. As Grace drove along, she could not still Velma's voice in her mind.

"It was right mean and nasty," she had told Grace. "Alma went on and on about how Sarina was a Muslim. Frank argued she wasn't, then when he couldn't change her mind, he said for her to think what she liked, just to keep it to herself. He said the church board didn't want to lose Pastor Denny, and they didn't give a hoot who Denny married so long as she was Christian. He reminded Alma that Sarina was studying to convert and would soon be baptized. She was a good choice for Denny, since she'd already made her home in Covington. I thought Frank was very reasonable, but Alma sure didn't. She's never reasonable. Lordy Lord, it was like the devil took ahold of Alma. She started screaming, yelling, and pitching things."

Suddenly Grace realized how close she was to the car in front of her and slowed, then sped up again and passed the car. Her speedometer read seventy-five, and she slowed down, once more hearing Velma's voice, high-strung and agitated.

"Alma was flinging stuff, and I could hear glass breaking. Then it got real nasty, real personal and mean, and I heard Frank threaten her."

"Threaten her, how?" Grace had asked. She noticed now that she had gone from a cruising speed of sixty to seventy-five again, and again Grace slowed her car. But her mind kept straying from the road to Velma, who seemed to have enjoyed Frank and Alma's fight.

"Lord, Grace, I never heard the likes of it. Frank shriek-ing at her, 'Dammit, Alma, you were born a bitch, mean through and through.'"

Grace glanced down at her watch, noted that she was late, switched to the left lane, and zoomed past several cars. Her tires seemed to have sprouted wings, and Grace heard Velma's voice rising higher and higher.

"Alma cursed him! Foul, foul language, too foul to re-peat. That Alma's always been mean-spirited. They went at it then, verbally hitting one another below the belt." Velma had lowered her voice. "Frank said he wished he'd never married her, that he'd never loved her, and Alma screamed that sleeping next to him in bed repulsed her, made her sick to her stomach."

Grace felt the car tremble. Leaning forward, she gripped the wheel harder as she zipped past another car. "Why are they all driving so slowly?" She looked at her speedometer and her heart raced. She was way over the speed limit. Grace's foot hit the brake hard. Her car spun out of control and she heard the grind of metal on metal as she careened off the highway into the guardrail, bending and tearing the metal on the median. Her air bags opened with a thud, striking her chest and face hard, blocking the light and her vision. Grace pitched sideways, thumping her head against the doorframe. Everything went black.

✿✿

AN AMBULANCE BORE GRACE to the emergency room at Mission Memorial Hospital. Once she was identified, the hospital phoned Roger in South Carolina. Roger phoned Bob immediately, but when a distraught Bob arrived at the hospital, they refused to allow him to see Grace.

"Are you the next of kin?" the woman behind the desk asked.

Bob shook his head. "No, she's my companion of many years. It's the same as if we were married."

The woman checked her computer, then looked up at Bob. Her son, the next of kin, has been notified. He's on his way. You'll have to wait until he gets here to see her." She turned from Bob to answer the telephone.

Bob waited until she had hung up. "At least tell me how she is? Is she badly hurt? Do you know what happened?"

"That information will have to wait until Mr. Singleton arrives," the woman said, not unkindly but without empathy.

Bob grabbed the edge of the desk with both hands and leaned forward. "Her son, Roger, is driving up from South Carolina. It's going to take him a good hour and a half to get here. Grace, Mrs. Singleton, is alone and I want to know how she is. I want to see her."

To her credit, the woman did not order him out or call a security guard to escort him out. She regarded him from behind the high desk and shook her head. "I'm very sorry, sir, but I don't make policy. Why don't you wait in the waiting room?" She nodded to her left. "There's coffee and magazines." Then she turned her full attention to a woman who had approached the desk and was inquiring about her family member.

Bob released the edge of the desk. How *dare* this woman prevent him from being with Grace! Angry and feeling helpless, Bob walked away, his frustration and sense of helplessness increasing. He must call someone, talk to someone. Who? Amelia was in Connecticut. Hannah would be as upset and as frustrated as he was at not being able to see Grace. Ah—Denny Ledbetter would lend a sympathetic ear without getting upset. Bob reached in his pocket for his cell phone and came up empty. *Stupid me. I left it right there on my dresser.*

Bob slipped coins into a pay phone and lifted the receiver, then stared at the number pad, his mind blank. He set the phone on its cradle and sank into the closest chair. *Think, you know this phone number. What is it, darn it?* He brought a fist down on his knee and suddenly remembered. Reaching for the phone, he inserted money again and dialed Denny.

On the first ring, Denny picked up.

Bob choked up, and tears spilled from his eyes. "Denny, I called because . . ." He stopped, unable to continue for a moment. "Grace's been hurt in an accident, a car crash. I'm at Mission Hospital."

"I'll come right over. I can be there in a half hour."

"No need to come. Her son's on his way. I just had to talk with someone." Bob stifled a sob and placed his hand over the phone. He'd best get a grip on himself, and people were looking at him. Bob straightened his shoulders and related what little he knew. When the phone service voice indicated he needed more money to continue talking, he inserted additional coins. "Grace was driving. Yes, it was her car. No, I have no idea how she is. No, they won't let me see her—only family. I'm going nuts, waiting for Roger to get here."

"I know that rule. I'm so sorry, Bob. Roger will be there soon."

"I don't know where she is, if she's having surgery, how she is. Denny, what am I gonna *do*?" Bob stared out of the glass windows at the end of the room, seeing nothing. "Dear Lord, Denny, what if she's . . ." He stopped, unable to go on. The voice inserted itself again, informing him that his time was up.

"Trust in the Lord," Denny offered. "It's going to be all

right. Grace is in His hands, and Mission has very fine doctors."

"Pray for Grace, Denny—and for me, too." Bob hung up, walked slowly away, and slumped into a chair away from other people. *I've survived a horrendous war, yet I feel as if I'm gonna come apart. Pray for me, Denny.* Bob choked back tears.

Time passed slowly, the hands of the clock on the far wall lumbering from minute to minute. Bob's eyes traveled across the pages of a racing car magazine, a hiking magazine, a gardening magazine, *National Geographic,* when Roger finally arrived, looking as distracted as Bob felt.

Together, they stood at the same desk before the same woman, who was all smiles. "The doctors are waiting to talk with you, Mr. Singleton."

They followed a young volunteer down a hallway into a small sterile office. Moments later a tall, middle-aged physician entered, shook their hands, introduced himself, and got right down to business. "Mrs. Singleton suffered a concussion when she struck her head. She's broken her leg, which is in a cast, and she suffered lacerations of the face and arms from the air bag. Having gotten your permission on the phone, Mr. Singleton, we set and put a cast on her leg.

"Because of the concussion, we'd like to keep her overnight. If all goes well, as I'm sure it will, you can take her home tomorrow afternoon. You may now see her briefly, one at a time. She needs to rest."

Roger and Bob stood in the doorway of Grace's room. The cast on her leg went to her knee and there was a knob on the bottom to make walking easier. A tiny line of stitches spread across her chin where she'd sustained a deep gash; otherwise Grace seemed fine. Delighted to see them, she extended her arms to embrace them both.

"They want to keep me overnight because of the blow to my head. I was unconscious when the paramedics got to me. But see, I'm fine. I can even walk with this cast. I want to go home."

Bob's stomach lurched. He knew the danger of head injuries from his army experience. "It's best you stay overnight," he said. "I'll stay here with you, if they'll let me."

"We'll arrange for you to stay," Roger said.

"I'm fine, Roger. You go back home. I'm so sorry you had to rush up here like this."

"He wouldn't have had to, if they'd have let me see you and be with you," Bob said.

"Why wouldn't they?" Grace asked.

"I'll explain it when you get home," Bob said. "Lie back

and try to sleep. You may feel fine, but you've had a major shock to your system and you need to rest."

"I could use a cup of coffee," Roger said. "How about we go to the cafeteria, Bob?"

Grace closed her eyes. Bob was right, of course. She was relieved not to have had major injuries, but under her bravado lurked exhaustion. Grace felt her body sink into lethargy and her eyes closed. "Go on," she mumbled. "I'm tired."

In the cafeteria, the men had coffee and sandwiches. Bob said, "Grace and I are as married as a married couple, in every sense except legally. You have no idea how many times I've proposed." He shook his head. "This whole business of my not being allowed to see her . . ." His fists clenched. "What if she'd been seriously injured, in a coma, or dying? Roger, I don't think I can go through something like this again."

"How can I help? I'm not sure I have that kind of influence with my mother. She can be mighty stubborn."

"Don't I know it. Seems she and the girls have some kind of pact that they won't leave one another, that they'll be there for one another to the end. It's a noble sentiment, if they didn't have any other family."

"Maybe if you explain how they treated you here, how you felt, Mother would change her mind," Roger suggested.

Bob sighed. "I can try again."

When they returned to the room, Grace was asleep, and the nurse suggested that they go home, since she was sedated and would probably sleep through the night.

"You'll keep a good watch on her?" Bob asked.

"Of course we will."

AFTER REACHING DENNY, BOB had phoned Hannah to tell her about the accident.

Hannah felt the blood drain from her face and reached for the chair at her desk to keep from falling, then sank into it. Grace in an accident? Grace hurt and Bob couldn't see her? Then she would not be able to see her, either. They must all sit on their hands, worry, and wait for Roger to get there from South Carolina—outrageous! What kind of cruel rule was that?

Hannah took several deep breaths to calm herself, then left Bella's Park and hurried down the road to Cove Road Church. Settling into the pew in the front of the church, she lowered her head and prayed softly. "Lord, I don't visit you often. Forgive me for that. I need your help now, please. My dearest friend, Grace—you know how good she is, how kind. She's been in a car accident. Please take care of her, and heal whatever injuries she's sustained. Make her well, hale and hearty, please. *Please.*" Her voice cracked, and she wept, her body shaking.

That evening, Amelia phoned to say that she and Milo would be returning the next day. Hannah decided it was best not to tell her about Grace's accident. What could Amelia do but worry? Please God, Grace would be home by the time Amelia returned.

SITTING ALONE IN PRAYER in a rear pew, Pastor Denny had seen Hannah enter. It had touched him deeply to witness the usually irreligious Hannah bowed in prayer, and he had slipped quietly away rather than cause her any embarrassment or jar her communion with the Lord.

26

God's Grace

GRACE WAITED EAGERLY FOR Roger and Bob to
arrive the next morning, waited anxiously for the
doctor to come and give the order that she could
be discharged. As she waited, she reviewed the
accident in her mind and berated herself for her
carelessness, for not paying attention to the road,
her speed, other cars. *Thank God I was in the left
lane and crashed into the guard rail instead of into
another car, injuring or even killing someone.* She
shuddered. How terrible that would have been.
How fortunate she had been. Her broken leg
would heal, as would the bruises and cuts.

A nurse appeared in the door, smiled at Grace, took her pulse, blood pressure, and temperature. She nodded. "You seem fit and ready to leave us."

"Thank you for your good care," Grace said. Everyone had been kind—the medics who pulled her from her car, the medic who sat beside her in the ambulance, his eyes reassuring, his touch gentle. The doctor in the emergency room had tended to her promptly. He, too, had been kind. She'd been x-rayed and prodded, her leg set in a cast. They had done a CAT scan of her head and found no bleeding or swelling, someone had said.

One thing bothered her. In the emergency room, she had asked for Bob, given his phone number to someone, and had been told that her son was on his way. *Fine,* she'd thought, *but I want Bob.* They had sedated her, and when she awoke in a hospital room, Bob and Roger were standing over her bed. Soon they would be here to take her home.

Now, at her request, the nurse handed Grace a mirror. Grace stared at her face. "I look ghastly. I had no idea I had that many bruises and all those stitches on my chin. No wonder it hurts to open my mouth. And my eyes are black and blue, as if someone socked me smack between them." She dropped the mirror onto her lap.

"The plastic surgeon who attended you is the best. The

stitch scars will fade; you'll hardly see them." The nurse took Grace's hand. "Mrs. Singleton, your entire system has sustained a shock. Air bags save lives, but they also pack quite a wallop. In time you'll feel like your old self, but give it time. I suggest you treat your body almost like a separate self."

Grace looked at her, puzzled.

"Every organ in your body was jarred in the accident. Your body needs you to allow it to heal—not to rush it, or push it. If you're tired, rest. It will take longer to heal if you stress yourself and do too much." She smiled and patted Grace's hand. "We all want to get up and get going, get back to our old selves. Just give it time."

Grace lay back against the pillows. The nurse was right, of course. "Thanks for reminding me. I'll remember your words every time I want to force myself to get up and go, or when I feel frustrated because it's happening too slowly, or I worry that I ought not to be tired."

Then Grace asked, "Do you have a comb or brush? I'd like to fix myself the best I can before Bob and my son get here."

The nurse opened the drawer beside the bed and brought out a brush, comb, lipstick, and other cosmetics. "Mr. Richardson brought these last evening after you'd fallen asleep. He thought you'd want them."

Grace smiled, feeling warm inside. "Bob's like that. He takes good care of me." She picked up the mirror again. Her hair stuck out at odd angles about her face. "I look a mess," she muttered, and with great effort brushed the hair from her forehead. Ouch, but it hurt her side to stretch, hurt to lift her arm. *This is going to take time, lots of time.* She took the lipstick the nurse handed her and colored her lips. *That's a little better.*

27

Bob's Angst

Since the accident, Bob's nights had been sleepless. He spent them pacing the floor, remembering how he had been kept from Grace, not knowing how badly she'd been hurt, imagining the worst. He hadn't mentioned this to Grace but had told Max, who suggested that Bob ask his doctor for sleeping pills or tranquilizers. But Bob had seen too many veterans struggling to get their lives back, to free themselves of addiction, and he did not take drugs.

"I've lived through worse," he told Max, and he reminded himself of that later as he paced the floor. But the lack of sleep was getting to him.

He'd never loved anyone as much as he loved Grace. In that hospital, waiting helplessly, facing the possibility of her having permanent injuries or even dying, had literally undone this tough old soldier.

Now he found himself dozing whenever he sat in a chair, and struggling to keep his eyes open when driving his car. His son, Russell, had invited him to stay at his home with him and his grandchildren. But Tyler, a teenager, whose mother had been killed in a car accident, had literally collapsed on the floor sobbing at the news of the accident. Five-year-old Melissa, from whose mother Russell was divorced, went to pieces when Tyler fell apart. She had flung herself on top of him and wept as if her little heart were broken. Bob had felt even more exhausted, and it had taken a good hour to calm the children.

Bob stayed there for one night. Tyler's mournful face and Melissa's childish questions about Grace's accident were more stressful than being alone at home. So, he paced the floor and worried when she would regain her energy, her vitality, her zest for life. An accident like this and the mental trauma could take years off her life. *Years!* The thought terrified him; the idea that he could be alive and she would not be with him brought paroxysms of tears.

Be glad Grace is alive and that she's going to be all right, he told himself. But his irrational mind, like some cruel jailer, sprang alive at night to torment him. He lay awake and worried, and relived the anger he had felt at not being allowed to see Grace or know how she was until Roger's arrival.

He had always wanted to marry Grace. Year after year he had proposed, to no avail. Grace, Hannah, and Amelia had found one another at the lowest point in their lives, at a time when they felt abandoned by their families. Their lives, their futures had seemed washed up and without meaning or purpose. They had bonded then, and made a commitment to share a home and care for one another as if they were family, and they had done that, irrespective of the fact that Hannah found Amelia exceedingly annoying at times. They *were* a family: they fussed and fumed about one another, but didn't let anyone else do so.

Then Hannah married Max, but she didn't really live with him. Most nights she slept at the ladies' farmhouse. If you checked her closets in both houses, he bet you'd find most of her clothes at the farmhouse. Apparently, this arrangement worked for Max.

Would *he* be satisfied with the same? Bob shook his head. He wanted Grace with him in the living room in the evenings, beside him in bed at night.

Well, he'd deal with all of this when she was well. He'd tell her what had transpired at the hospital, and how frustrated and helpless he had felt, unable to be with her when she needed him most. That might change her mind.

These feelings persisted though he hid them for weeks after Grace came home.

ONE EVENING, AFTER DINNER at the ladies' farmhouse and visiting with Grace, he asked her, "Have anything good to read that I can take home?"

"Why not take one of the diaries? I think you'd find them interesting." She handed him the diary at the top of the pile. "Tom wrote this," she said.

Isn't he harder to read than John?"

"Yes, but I think you'll find this one very interesting."

Bob took the small book, kissed her good night, then drew his jacket about him and hurried across the lawns to his cottage. After a hot shower and a last cup of decaffeinated coffee, he settled into bed with the diary.

"We was a-fightin' all day and night and when it was done, the captain said we'd done took back land south of Virginia, cotton country with big ole plantation houses, them Yanks spared so as they could live in 'em like they was kings.

Nights was cold, and I done billeted in a barn full up with sacks of cottonseed, and I made me a bed of 'em sacks. I was a-settlin' in when I heard me a-moanin' comin' from a wall I was facin'. I heard it ag'in, moanin' and a-bangin' 'guinst the wall, like to scare me to my grave. After a time, I eased 'round that wall. It weren't no wall but a pen that got a gate and lock.

"Marse, I beggin' you, let me out," a voice said.

"Who be you? How you get in there?"

"Ole Missy," she said, "I done catch and stew me a chicken to feed my ailin' mother and my children."

"Who put you in there?"

"Marse Henderson, suh. He say he own de chickens, and I ain't to have none. I figure he own de chicken, he own me, so I could have food to feed my mother and children."

I hankered to know if this Marse, as she called him, was one of us or one of them. So I asked her what color jacket her Marse wore, an she says it's blue, and *he come with plenty horses and men and guns and chase off the old Marse and took the house.*

A damned Yank, I thought, not feedin' a slave and treatin' her worse than her master would have. And the Yanks say they come to free the slaves. A rage rose up in me, and I took my rifle butt and broke that there lock, and she done fall out on the ground, tall and skinny, ribs stickin' out her chest, eyes big and scared. I gave her some of my rations, salt pork and a few potatoes. The woman thanked me and walked away. I ain't never laid eyes on her ag'in.

Next day we find the room the captain was a-lookin' fer, where they gins cotton. All was left there was this light white stuff a-coverin' the floor and it done fly up in our faces when we walk on it. Captain was a-yellin' to get out of there, and we run like foxes out that place and jumped in a creek nearby. Our clothes were wet then, and it was mighty cold in our billets that night.

Bob turned the pages reading more of the soldier's war experiences:

They brung um in, some was wounded men, some was dyin', faster than we could tend 'em. We strawed the floor thick 'neath the tables to catch the blood where the doctors was a-cuttin' and sawin', but afore you could chew and spit tobacco, that straw was a-soakin' with blood and slippery.

I done hold the chloroform to their faces to ease the pain and bring on sleep. Sawed off limbs we pitch in a corner to bury later. One time, a foot flyin' by slapped me in my face, spreadin' blood, and I retched.

Another section dealt with vermin, lice, chiggers, mosquitoes:

Hell was mosquitoes. They give us nettin', one time, and we hung it above us in our tents 'til somebody's candle done set the nettin' afire and we all went a-runnin' from that tent and sat in the cold and watched our worldly goods burn. One night when the guns was still, I hear the sound of a fiddle from the Yank's camp. It was sweet, and for a time I close my eyes and try to forget the fightin'.

❧❧

And so it went, page after page. It made Bob ill to read, so he left his bed and went into the living room to his desk, where he opened a drawer and drew out a small velvet-covered box containing his Purple Heart. As he stared at this symbol of his bravery his mind snapped back to the horrors of that Vietnam night: dark, cold, helicopters overhead dropping fiery death—the noise of it, the blood of it, the horror of it, the sloughing through mud, the screams. Wounded, he somehow found the strength to carry a young soldier, a mere boy, out from under that fire to safety.

He had never spoken of this to his son Russell, or to Martin, or even to Grace, to anyone. Every Christmas Bob received a card from that boy, a man now with a grown family. They had moved several times, and the address was always neatly printed on the envelope. Bob had thrown the cards away and never returned the greeting. He'd done what anyone would have done and needed no ongoing reminder or praise. As he closed the box, Bob suddenly hoped that he would get a card again this year. He'd behaved foolishly. This year he'd return the greeting, send back a card and tell of his life in Covington, of Grace.

Grace. Bob thought again of the hospital, of his feeling

of helplessness, of how many times in war he had felt that overwhelming sense of helplessness. His jaw clenched, and the muscles in his back and arm tensed. How dare those hospital people treat him, a war hero awarded the Purple Heart, like that? Exhausted, Bob closed the drawer. For a time he sat there, too tired to move, then he rose and shuffled to his bedroom, where he fell onto his bed. Moments later, he was asleep.

28

Planning a Celebration

HANNAH'S VOICE ROSE CRISP and harsh. Too harsh, she realized, as the words came out. "We have to start thinking about this Christmas celebration *you* cooked up." Sitting behind her desk, she faced Amelia, who stood across from her.

"Don't look at me as if I'm some miscreant schoolgirl who's about to be expelled," Amelia retorted. Turning, she walked to the door, then stopped. *If this matter weren't so urgent, I'd walk out of this office, and to heck with Hannah and her high-and-mighty attitude.*

What was wrong with Hannah, anyway? These

last months she'd been more critical than usual of anything Amelia had done or said. It hadn't always been like this, and this had to stop. Emboldened by her growing anger, Amelia turned and strode to the desk, leaned forward, and glared at Hannah.

"I am sick and tired of the way you talk to me, Hannah. We're different, but that doesn't make you better than me. I know that you're a much better organizer than I am. We've been sharing a home for years now, and lately you're overly critical of me: things that never bothered you about me suddenly do." She scowled. "I'd attribute it to menopause, but we're all way past that. If something's bothering you, don't take it out on me."

"I am sorry, Amelia," Hannah said. "You're right. I've had things on my mind, and I probably have taken them out on you."

Amelia stared at Hannah, an apology being the last thing she'd expected. "Probably? You *have* taken it out on me. What do you mean? You're going to change now? You're going to treat me with respect, and not like some naughty child you can't abide? If you do that, how will you handle your frustrations? Who else will you take them out on? Who else would be foolish enough to sit and take your criticism?"

Hannah rose and came to where Amelia stood. "Please

don't go. Come sit with me on the couch and let me explain."

Grudgingly, Amelia moved toward the couch. "We agreed this celebration would be a nice thing to do. It's not my fault that Grace was hurt in an accident. She's getting around with her cast just fine now."

Hannah sank onto the couch, set her elbows on her knees, and dropped her head into her hands. When she lifted her head, there were tears in her eyes. She brushed them away with the balls of her hands. "I'm so sorry, Amelia. I've been worried sick about Max."

Immediately, Amelia reached out for Hannah's hand. "Is something wrong with him?"

There, she had finally said it aloud. And of all people, to Amelia. "He's overly tired lately. I see him walking up the hill so slowly, every step seems to be a huge effort. He blames it on age and hides out here on this couch. Taking a nap, he calls it, but his naps go on for hours. I think he should have a thorough exam, but I can't get him to go to a doctor. I took my fears out on you, and I am so sorry. Can you forgive me?"

"Of course I forgive you," Amelia said in a small voice. She looked away. "Hannah, have you considered that Max may be depressed? He's made a huge change in his life, selling the dairy; Max loved his cows. And then all that trauma with Zachary being so horrible to him and then just taking off."

"I really hadn't. I was focused on a physical ailment, but maybe you're right. He won't talk about that awful scene with Zachary and closing the dairy. Never would." She looked at Amelia and smiled. "Thanks, Amelia. You've given me a good insight. I haven't done anything but worry about him and Grace."

"Grace is doing great. Even with a cast on she can help. She's been making phone calls, licking invitation envelopes, things like that."

Hannah squeezed Amelia's hand. "When her accident happened, I missed you so much. It brought home to me our ages, our vulnerability." She sat back on the couch. "And all because of that awful Alma."

Amelia looked puzzled. "What's she got to do with Grace's accident? Was she in the car with her?"

"Velma told Grace about an awful argument Frank and Alma had, and Grace was thinking about it and paying no attention to the road."

Suddenly Amelia felt little and insignificant. She took a deep breath and blinked. They hadn't told her any of this. She wanted so much to be liked and needed, and they hadn't told her any of this.

Amelia felt like crying, but she wouldn't break down in front of Hannah. Besides, Hannah and Grace *had* needed her, whether they knew it or not. And they needed her now even more, to pull this party together, and she could do it.

Hannah was explaining how it had started with Denny's letter inviting everyone to Sarina's baptism and announcing their engagement. "I'm sure you got a letter, too, Amelia. It must be in that pile of mail at home in the basket in the kitchen."

Amelia's mind clouded. Had she seen that basket? She couldn't recall. If she had, she hadn't bothered to go through it. She'd been too concerned about Grace, too eager to return to the loop, to feel a part of things again.

Hannah continued, telling Amelia about Velma and Alma's conversation at the diner, about Charlie talking with Frank, and filled out the story of Frank and Alma's terrible below-the-belt fight, which had been heard by Velma.

So *this* was it! This was at the root of that nagging feeling Amelia had that she was outside of things, that there was some big secret she didn't know about. Only it wasn't a secret; they just hadn't bothered to tell her, though she'd been home for weeks. She was indeed out of the loop.

A deep sense of hurt spread through Amelia's chest. "Why didn't anyone tell me about all of this? Oh, but I'm being oversensitive, right?" Sarcasm filled her voice. "Why tell silly, foolish Amelia? What good would she be in a crisis?"

"That's not true; Bob called you right away. And Grace was so glad to see you—we all were." Hannah lifted her hands and dropped them in a gesture of giving up. "I am sorry, Amelia. I can only say that we've all been so absorbed in our own stuff. . . . I guess we simply forgot about Denny's letter and Alma, what with everything else going on."

Then Hannah's shoulders fell, and when she spoke, she sounded very tired. "Everyone's been upset and concerned about Grace, and I had this thing with Max on my mind. I pressed him to see a doctor, and *we* had our first big fight." Hannah choked up and looked away. Finally, she said, "This isn't the time for us to be arguing. We have to get this reunion of the relatives organized. We have to work together, Amelia. Tell me, please, how many of Milo's relatives are coming from Connecticut?"

Amelia sprang from the couch. "How can you turn it off like that?" She bent over and snapped her fingers in Hannah's face. "It's over, Amelia? You're feeling devastated, but forget about that and let's get on with business?" Amelia considered leaving, forgetting this whole reunion, going home and sulking. But it was too late to forget, and sulking would accomplish nothing.

She looked down at Hannah. "There are two couples coming and the daughter and grandson of one of the couples. Six people from Connecticut. I've made reservations for them at the Comfort Inn in Mars Hill. Are you satisfied, Hannah, or should you call the Comfort Inn and double check? After all, maybe I didn't do it right."

Hannah let out a breath. "Well done, Amelia. I have the South Carolina list sitting on my desk." She rose and walked to her desk for a notepad. "Roger said there are twelve coming from Walhalla. Two older couples, two younger couples, and four teenagers."

Amelia's anger drained away. Hannah had apologized. Max was ill with heaven only knew what. Grace was limited in what she could do. She and Hannah must work together if there was to be a holiday celebration. This meant a lot to the families soon to be reunited, and to herself and Grace and Hannah. They had pulled off quite a coup.

Amelia walked to Hannah's desk and held out her hands. Peace?"

Hannah took Amelia's hands in hers. "Peace."

Then Amelia counted on her fingers. "Milo and his family are eleven. He's managed to convince his father and uncle, who don't like anyone from up North, to come to the luncheon. Then there are Tom's relatives here, that professor Matthew Evans from Warren Wilson College. He called and left a message on Grace's machine that he's rounded up a total of thirteen relatives who all want to come, besides him and his wife and two sons. So that makes seventeen."

Bending over the desk, Amelia punched in the numbers on Hannah's adding machine. "That's a total of forty-six relatives plus us. There are six of us, including Mike. He should be back by then . . . oh, and Sarina and Denny makes eight."

"Don't forget my daughter Laura and her husband Hank, and Bob's son Russell and most likely Tyler. That makes twelve. If we think of anyone else, we can add them," Hannah said.

Amelia tapped the desk with her fingers. "We'll have to include Brenda and Molly and her husband and Velma and Charlie. They've offered a lot of help with the decorations, transporting people, and whatever else comes up. That's another three, so that's sixteen of us from Covington." She punched away at the numbers. "Forty-seven, plus sixteen is sixty-three. Let's make it sixty-seven."

"What do you think about seventy?" Hannah asked.

Amelia nodded. "If you'll give me the names of the Mueller relatives from South Carolina, I'll call and give them the name of that motel and others in Asheville, if they prefer to be in the city."

"Great." Hannah handed Amelia the pad. "Here are the names and phone numbers of the Penningtons and Muellers. They can take it from there."

Amelia took the pad. "We're going to have quite a crowd." Her face grew animated. "Can you believe we had this idea and it's about to happen? I'm really excited." She smiled at Hannah. "I hope you are, too." When Hannah did not reply, Amelia asked, "Did you and Grace go down and meet the Muellers?"

"Grace and Bob went. I was swamped at the park and"—she hesitated and looked away for a moment—"and I didn't want Max to drive. As it turned out, they decided to stay over at Roger's place for a few nights so they could meet with both of those families. Nice people, Grace said." Hannah opened and shut a desk drawer, then opened another as if she were looking for something. "I must get back to work."

"Of course. I'll take care of this," Amelia said. "Don't worry about anything. We'll sit down as soon as you have time and make a list of what we each need to do." Amelia left and shut the office door softly behind her.

Hannah shoved back her chair, strode to the door, and locked it. Returning to her desk, she sat and opened the first drawer, which she had slammed shut so quickly, and removed one of Tom's diaries. When Grace was in the hospital, she had taken several of the diaries to her office, and each afternoon she read from one of them, randomly.

❦❦

I'm a-lyin' on clean sheets washed by Miss Ella Mae, bless her, and hung in the hot sweet summer sun to dry. And I'm thinkin' 'bout layin' in a tent so small a man of good height must bend his legs to sleep. This day my mind gone back to the war, to a day we done marched in rain and wind, and the enemy hidin' and shootin' at us, and nobody to say which way to go. It's a wonder anyone lived to tell 'bout it, for few of us survived and we ate what birds were a-layin' about, killed by shots fired. Still, we mustta had the upper hand, somehow, 'cause we picked up plenty of their loaded muskets as we went. They mustta dropped 'em and run. All I know for sure was one of our men was hit in the thigh with a ball, one lost a finger, and another took a ball in his cheek. I couldn't help 'em none 'cause I ain't had no medic trainin' yet. Seein' them sufferin' so's what turned my mind to learnin' about healin'.

Got to stop thinkin' 'bout this, or I'll be screamin' like John does at night. Best I roll over on my clean-smellin' sheets Miss Ella Mae washed for me, and say a prayer of thanks to the good Lord that he brung me to this place and kept me from dyin' from a ball from an enemy musket.

❧❦

There was a long blank space in the journal before Tom continued, and from what came next, Hannah assumed that many days had passed.

> Got to thinkin' 'bout the day a battalion of Union men took ten of our men prisoner. I never did know who they was and wondered if any of 'em was a buddy of mine, Matt or Sammy—just a boy, Sammy. I remember findin' me a place away from the others and beatin' a tree with a stick, I hated war so bad. I couldn't see no sense in my ever joinin' up. None of it makes no sense no more. I coulda deserted but I seen 'em shoot a deserter. First thing they made him do was build his own coffin. Then they sat him down on it and ten men there a-standin' there, pointin' rifles at him. They shot him dead. I seen him throw his hands in the air, seen his body jerk, and seen him fall back into that coffin. I never went to church much back home, but I sure did pray a lot then, prayed for Lord Jesus to bring me safe home with all my limbs. And He done take care of me, bringin' me safe here with Miss Ella Mae, God bless her.
> It was John pushed me to write 'bout all this.

Sometimes he helps me with words. He's smart, that John, knows his words. Come evenin' all summer long he's a-sittin' on a log by that old tree, writin' away, and come winter he's a-sittin' on his bed burnin' a candle writin'. Says it rests his mind.

She turned a page and sighed with satisfaction, having found the section she liked.

Today I done meet Glory Ann Hendricks. Husband got hisself killed fellin' trees to clear his land. Glory was named just right. I was lookin' at her in Miss Aron's store, kinda plump, which suits me fine, copper hair a-shinin' in the sun like gold itself.

Miss Ella Mae done send me to Miss Aron's for canned stewed apples and other things. Miss Ella Mae tasted them apples at Miss Maggie's house and took a fancy to 'em. When I seen Glory, I near to forget what I come for. Glory smiled at me, and my mouth clamped shut. She gonna think me an idiot like Issy, 's what I was a-thinkin', standin' there just a-lookin' at her.

Glory's got her a bold character. She walked herself up to me and says how she's right glad to meet me.

She asked if my name was Tom and says how she's heard how good I is to Miss Ella Mae and how glad she is the old lady ain't havin' to live alone up in them mountains.

I nodded my head and kept a-noddin' 'til Miss Aron catch my eye and shake her head. Anyways, that's how we come to meet, me and Glory, and next day Glory done brung her three little girls to visit Miss Ella Mae, but all the while she's there, she's a-lookin' at me and talkin' to me 'bout how good the place lookin' and how she likes the room John and me built on to the cabin afore John got hisself married up with his Jenny. She says she and Jenny is good friends.

That Glory can laugh. A person can hear her laugh up and down the mountains. I was thinkin' she could make the birds sing, when she asked me to walk with her to the creek. Miss Ella Mae was a-dozin' in her chair. So, I got me up and walked with Glory to that there creek, and it was like she had a key to unlock my mouth, and I talk more un I talk in years. We started meetin' up at church, and afore you know it, I done asked her to marry up with me, and I promise to care for her girls like they was mine.

Well, then I was thinkin' where I was gonna put this here crowd a people. I sure wasn't gonna leave Miss

Ella Mae. Miss Ella Mae say we could build plenty more rooms on the cabin. John, and me, and folks we done meet since the war end, all of us feel like we belongs to this here mountain, as we is Miss Ella Mae's kin, an' they done come and work with us, cuttin' and shapin' trees for the walls and floor. We got us a fine big cabin, now, with a cookin' an eatin' part to itself. Miss Ella Mae got a room for herself, but after a time she make us bring her bed back in that there kitchen. Bed, rocker, and cloth box for makin' quilts. And that old hog gun went back up over the fireplace. Old folks like things how they are. Change ain't easy for 'em's what I figure.

Anyways, we done finish the cabin and married up, Glory and me, and after church we roast a pig in the yard and had us a big ole party. Issy brung his friend Joe with his fiddle, and we sing and dance 'til the big ole red moon took hisself to bed over that there hill.

Hannah smiled. This was what they wanted for Tom. A wife, a good life, and it sounded as if he had found that. She regretted that the diaries and letters stopped shortly after the men married, but that probably meant that they had finally put the war behind them and moved on to better, happier lives.

Hannah shut the diary and turned her chair. With the window closed she was unable to hear the hammering and sawing on the hillside, but she could see Max. In the past he'd be up and about, directing everything. Now he was sitting under a tree in the shade. That worried her. As she watched, Max rose from his chair and walked to where the men were hammering. *Ah, good,* Hannah thought, *he's feeling better.*

Her thoughts returned to the diary and Tom. What horror he had seen, and what hell he had lived through. Was Amelia right? Were destinies written? Why did Tom and John survive so many battles, when so many others had been killed? Why had Miss Ella Mae Evans come along and saved their lives? She could have located her grandson at a far end of that field, buried him, and been on her way. She could have seen the two men in a ditch and walked right on past them. Hannah gave herself the reply she would give Amelia—why ask questions to which there are no answers?

Hannah sat, her hands loose in her lap, and thought how good it was that they would soon reunite Tom and John's family members and present the diaries to them. While Grace was still in the hospital, Hannah had checked Grace's answering machine and had returned a call from Professor Matthew Evans. He and his wife came to the house and read the diaries and letters of his ancestor, and had been fascinated. Matthew's wife, Maria, cried, and now they would be there along with their children and cousins from Georgia and South Carolina.

Hannah couldn't imagine parting with the diaries and letters. She hadn't realized how attached she'd become to them, how important they were, and how sitting together reading them had brought Grace, Amelia, and herself the warmth and companionship of earlier days in Covington. They couldn't give them to the families. Wouldn't it be better to give them copies, and to turn the diaries and letters over to a Civil War organization that preserved memorabilia? She must discuss this with Amelia and Grace. They could each keep copies, too. Why hadn't she thought of that before?

Hannah picked up one of John's diaries and opened it randomly to a page in the middle.

> *My bones surely ache tonight. We worked all day clearing a field, hauling and carrying off stumps. Miss Ella Mae has a fine parcel of land, but much of it was never cleared for pasture for cows and horses. Being so tired takes my mind back to soldiering and long*

*marches, and to one time when a halt was called. We
were never told when they would call a halt. It could
be a long halt with food and rest, or a short halt, but
when this one was called my corps melted off to the
sides of the road, and I found a piece of a hayfield, lay
back on my knapsack, and shut my eyes, wishing I was
home.*

*Next thing I knew, we were ordered up. I couldn't
move for being stiff as a board. I'd have died there, if
not for my buddies pulling me to my feet, setting my
knapsack on my back, and shoving me in line. Those
times, I wished I had never joined up, that I had
heeded my pa and stayed with Emily, adjusted, like Ma
called it, to life with a feather head. She sure didn't like
Emily. Well, it's turned out for the best, my being here
now with my Jenny, and I thank the Lord every day as
I cut these trees to clear new pastureland.*

Hannah returned the diary to her drawer and rose from
her desk. No time to think any more about this now. It was
time to call Denny. The celebration lunch on Christmas
Day at the church was being catered, and she had told
Denny that she and Max would rent the plates, silverware,
and glasses, plus any additional tables needed. That way
everything would match, and the ladies in charge of the

monthly church suppers wouldn't argue among themselves about how many of what there were or who had put what where. *Would* they need extra tables and chairs?

And who was in charge of decorating the hall? Amelia was great at decorating, and she'd have lots of help. Grace would do what she could—she could sit in a chair if need be and tell Bob what to do.

And Hannah realized that she was finally enjoying these preparations.

29

Grace

It was Christmastime and Grace was still in her cast, though getting about with a sturdy cane. They had had several small snow showers, and folks talked of a white Christmas. Even the weatherman suggested that maybe, just maybe, they would have snow on the twenty-fifth.

Grace sat on her porch and watched her neighbors string lights on their porches. It frustrated her not to be able to climb a ladder and help Russell, Tyler, Melissa, Sadie, Miriam, and Bob string the icicle lights around their porch.

She wanted to walk in the Asheville Mall to

see the store decorations. This year she'd have bought fewer gifts, with the price of everything so high. Instead, she had sent in an order to a catalog for small things, funny things, that she hoped would arrive on time.

She was delighted that Tom's and John's relatives were coming. The Muellers and Penningtons in Walhalla had heard from Roger about the accident and sent flowers to the house. Louise wrote that she and Ben were eager to see Grace and Bob again.

Grace felt fussed. She wanted to do her part, but what *was* that part? Everything seemed to have been taken care of.

Amelia had risen to the challenge and done a beautiful job decorating the church hall. She had come in one day, flushed and excited, and said, "We're having a star-filled-night theme, with one huge one to represent the star of Bethlehem." Amelia had pointed to the ceiling of their living room. "You wouldn't recognize that church hall. The ceiling's covered with tiny lights. Molly and Laura have enlisted all their friends to cut out tiny silver stars, which will go around the lights and the big star, too. Max had his men bring us a tall, fresh, beautiful Christmas tree, and we're going to use tiny old-fashioned candles like Tom and John did for Miss Ella Mae. Remember we read about that?

Grace nodded and wondered if Amelia had checked the fire code. She would ask Hannah, for she hadn't wanted to dampen Amelia's enthusiasm.

"Hannah ordered pale green tablecloths and pots of red poinsettias for every table," Amelia had said. "They came today, the tablecloths and the table settings. It's going to be so gorgeous, Grace! You'll love everything. Get Bob to bring you over to see what we're doing."

"I'll talk to him about it. He doesn't want me trying to go down steps alone."

So Grace buried her frustration at having to sit on the sidelines while Hannah, Amelia, Sarina, Molly, and Laura talked excitedly and planned the grand holiday celebration she had anticipated being a major part of. Instead, she'd argued with Bob.

"If you overdo it," he'd said, "that break will take much longer to heal. You're going to be back in the swing of things before you know it, honey. And don't forget, Hannah and Max are having everyone to José's Restaurant at Bella's Park on Christmas Eve for dinner. It'll be closed to customers, and give us a chance to meet everyone," Bob had said.

"I wanted to have them all here. I wanted to cook a turkey dinner for them," Grace had cried, and Bob had taken her into his arms and held her.

AT THIS MOMENT, WHILE the others hung lights, a breathless Amelia ran up the porch steps and took the rocker beside Grace. "I have news such news!"

"What? What is it?" Grace asked.

Amelia grinned. "You are not going to believe this."

"Well, *tell* me," Grace said.

Amelia pushed strands of hair from her face, which was rosy from exertion. "It's Alma. It seems she's had a conversion of sorts."

"A conversion?" Grace asked.

"Yes, she went to see Denny to apologize. Denny hadn't a clue about what she was apologizing for, and Alma caught herself in time and said she'd come to congratulate him on his engagement to Sarina and was apologizing for not coming sooner, what with the terrible accident and you being so dear to her."

"How do you know all of this?" Bob asked as he walked up the steps and took a chair beside Amelia. "A fly on the wall?"

Amelia's eyes twinkled. "You might say that. Ida McCorkle was visiting the pastor. She brings him flowers from her garden. I guess Alma didn't realize she was there, at first."

"Good old Ida," Bob said. "McCorkle Creek's best gossip. She and Alma are a pair."

"But I don't understand. What caused the change in Alma?" Grace said.

Amelia giggled, then covered her mouth with her hand. "It's no laughing matter, actually. After that dressing-down Frank gave Alma, she went to pieces, called in her sons, and they had a big family powwow. Her sons know the difference between a few terrorists and most Muslims and Hindus, and agreed with Frank that Alma was way out of line. Anyhow, there was another big scene, and Alma ended up taking back everything she'd said against Sarina. She apologized to Frank and went to see Denny, telling him she's all for his marriage to that sweet Sarina."

Grace wondered, had Alma really had a change of heart or was she playing a game to quiet Frank, avoid a divorce, and get things back to normal?

"Well, I'm glad she went to see Denny and congratulated him. We don't need chaos in this little congregation," Bob said.

Grace agreed, "This *is* good news, Amelia."

30

Preparing for a Christmas Celebration

ONE EVENING SOON AFTER, Grace and Amelia sat on the porch, bundled up in blankets and sipping hot tea. Amelia said, "I'm shivering, Grace. Let's go in."

Grace rose, pulled herself up, leaned against the porch railing, and gazed up at the sky. "For a winter day, it's lovely—such gorgeous white clouds and a deep blue sky. Don't you love a sky like this?" She followed Amelia into the house.

In the kitchen, Amelia said, "Let's go over the preparations for the relatives and the Christmas lunch, okay? I don't want you to feel left out of anything. Sit at the table, and I'll get my folders. Be right back." She hurried upstairs.

Grace sighed and sat. It frustrated her not to be more involved all these weeks. The jobs assigned her included folding napkins so they looked like Christmas trees, writing place cards for seating, and making phone calls. Reasonable enough after a broken leg, she supposed. Thank God the cast would come off soon and her leg would grow strong again.

Amelia returned and with a grunt set a large box onto a chair, removed several different-colored folders from the box, and laid them in a row on the table. She sat, placed her hands in front of her on the table, her fingers intertwined, and launched into an explanation of her filing system and of the contents of each folder. "Green, of course, is where I keep the bills. Yellow, being sunshiny, is where I keep correspondence from the relatives, which includes a record of phone calls made and received."

As she continued, Grace began to open and read the contents of one folder after the other. Amelia had outdone herself keeping things in order, easy to access and easy to understand. There were cars assigned to bring the relatives who needed transportation to and from José's Restaurant at Bella's Park where the first event would be held, then to the church for services Christmas morning, and so on.

Everyone would have name tags that stated where they were from and to which family they belonged. Tables were assigned to families and each table included one of the ladies, their men, or those who had worked most closely to make this celebration a reality: Russell, Laura and Hank, Molly, Brenda, Pastor Denny, and Sarina. Blue folders contained all anyone would need to know about decorating a room for a grand event.

Grace set the blue folder aside and looked out the window.

"Is something wrong? Did I overlook something?" Amelia asked.

"No, you've done a magnificent job. I was just thinking about the day when we all went to the church for Sarina's baptism." Grace set her elbows on the table and leaned forward. "And to see Alma in church smiling and hugging Sarina and Denny, wishing them well. I hope it's sincere."

Amelia straightened the row of folders. "Max made a video of the ceremony for Sarina to send home to her family. I hope it doesn't upset her father."

"Well, that's not our concern, is it?" Grace ran her hand lightly across the folders. "Look at all this work you've done—and so brilliantly!"

Amelia beamed, and they continued to speak about the parties.

31

Family Reunion

THEY ALL BEGAN TO arrive at Bella's Park at five in the evening. A light snow that afternoon had dusted the shrubs and every treetop, roof, and driveway. All along Cove Road, luminaries on lawns lent a soft, warm glow and enhanced the strings of tiny white bulbs decorating the porch of every home. The tall spruce growing on the lawn of Cove Road Church twinkled in its gown of white lights. The road seemed a veritable fairy-land to Grace as Bob helped her from home to Bella's Park.

The relatives arrived in pairs and in small and

large family groups, eager, bright-eyed, chattering nervously, and very curious about one another. At the door, the ladies were presented with corsages of poinsettias. Name tags were distributed to all. In the shadow of a tall Christmas tree, elegantly decorated with colored balls, the locals greeted and chatted with their formerly unknown relations.

It had been decided that copies of the diaries and letters, one set to each family group, would be presented to them on Christmas Day after the luncheon at the church. Grace had been chosen to read from John's and Tom's comments on their own past Christmases from their diaries.

As the conversations escalated, finger foods and glasses of wine punch were offered by uniformed servers.

Amelia watched Milo's uncle and father, oversized men with oversized personalities, interact graciously with their Yankee counterparts. The Connecticut families seemed enchanted, and Milo moved easily among them, his joy lighting the space like an aura about him.

Hannah approached Amelia and whispered, "I wanted you to know, I got Max to go to his doctor." She smiled.

"Good news?"

Hannah nodded. "The doctor did a blood panel, found no major illness, and found that what Max needed was iron, zinc, and some other vitamins. He gave Max shots right there. Max has been on the pills a few days now and feels better already."

"That's wonderful. It's a gift to you both on this holiday season," Amelia said.

Suddenly, Hannah looked serious. "Did you pick up the copies of the diaries and letters?"

A blank expression crossed Amelia's face. "Was I supposed to?"

"Yes, from Kinko's. You were supposed to pick them up yesterday. The originals are going to the Library of Congress, remember?"

Hannah had been polite and respectful, not the slightest bit sarcastic or critical since that day in her office. Now the old tone was back in Hannah's voice. Resentment and hurt swept over Amelia. For the world of her, she could not remember being asked to pick up those copies. If she had, she'd never have forgotten.

Amelia looked directly into Hannah's eyes. "I was never asked to do that." She leaned into Hannah, never taking her eyes off her face. "Think, Hannah. You've been distracted. Who *did* you ask to do this?"

Hannah took a step back. Her hand flew to her neck, and she seemed confused and flustered. "I don't know. Who did I ask, then?" Hannah seemed to shake herself as if she were casting off a light jacket.

"I'm sorry. I didn't mean to upset you, Amelia. I've been so worried about, well, you know." She reached for Amelia's hand. "Of course it wasn't you. I asked Max. He must have picked them up late yesterday. He's probably in the office wrapping them now. I'd best go find him, see if he needs help." She hurried away, leaving Amelia staring at her retreating figure, until animated conversations and laughter drew her into the mix seeking Milo.

The atmosphere in the dining room reminded Grace of an Irish pub—relaxed, jovial, and noisy, so loud at times she noted several people fumbling with their hearing aids, probably turning them down or off.

Snow fell steadily while they feasted, turning Covington into a winter wonderland. It was ten o'clock when they stepped from the building and made their way carefully down the snow-covered path to waiting cars.

Bob insisted that Grace wait inside while he went home and brought his car. He held her close as they made their way down the path, for snow had melted under the tread of many shoes and patches of ice had begun to form. At home in his cottage, Bob rubbed Grace's hands to warm them and brought her hot tea. Shoulder to shoulder, they sat on the sofa chatting about their experiences.

"It was splendid. A good time was had by all." He shook

his head. "Hard to believe you ladies pulled this off in so short a time."

"The credit goes to Amelia, Hannah, and all the others who helped them. Amelia really did most of it, Hannah told me. Besides helping the relatives with reservations and picking up the last-minute pieces, she organized the table decorations and corsages for tonight, and she's decorated the church hall for tomorrow's luncheon."

"In the army," Bob said, "I found that there were times when the least likely soldier performed in extraordinary ways."

"Yes." Grace rested her head on his shoulder, and he slipped his arm around her. "Amelia carried the ball on this one." She was silent a moment, then asked, "Hannah's been strange lately; have you noticed?"

"No wonder. Max told me he'd been feeling weak in the legs, hardly able to make it up the hill where they're doing construction, and he slept so much it scared the devil out of him. He was too scared to go see his doctor."

Astonished , Grace turned and looked at Bob. "Hannah never told me."

"I'm not surprised, what with all you've been through. I'm sure she didn't want to worry you."

"How is he? Is Max okay?"

Bob ran his hand across the top of Grace's head in a

soothing gesture. "He's gonna be fine. They did a complete physical and found that he's low in zinc and iron, B vitamins, stuff like that. Anyhow, they gave him vitamin B shots right off and pills, and he's already starting to feel better."

Grace brought her hands to her head. "Now I know what Amelia means when she complains about being left out of the loop. That's exactly how I feel."

"Take it easy, Gracie girl. It's gonna be okay. Just you rest your head back on this big old shoulder of mine, and let's sit and watch the fire in the fireplace. I put on some hickory logs. I like they way they burn, nice and slow."

He sat back, lifted his feet onto the hassock, and pulled Grace gently to him. "We have a big day tomorrow, honey. Talking to all those people can sure wear a person out."

Grace nodded agreement and snuggled against him.

THE NEXT DAY, SEATED in Cove Road Church, Grace turned to Bob. "Never have I seen this church packed like it is today. All of Covington must be here. They're curious to see the out-of-towners." Grace turned and nodded at Ida and her daughters, May and June, several rows away.

"Or so well decked out for Christmas," Bob said. "Look at the pews: every one of them has a garland on the end."

"Denny wanted to decorate the way they decorated churches in Connecticut in the mid-eighteen hundreds. See the ropes of evergreen and ivy entwined on the columns and on the railing where the choir stands, and all around the altar? That's part of it. And the candles are everywhere. I like not having the lights on. This service will be by candlelight."

"Look, Gracie." Bob pointed to a high stained-glass window. "Seems like they've got little shelves built to make the sills of every window wider, even the highest windows, and they're loaded with candles. Wow! That must have been a job."

Grace tucked her arm in Bob's. "Cozy and peaceful. I like it."

"You're going to read from the diaries about what past Christmases were like for John and Tom, right?" Bob asked.

"I'm scared to death, but yes, I agreed to stand at the pulpit if I can, and sit if I can't. Denny promised me a microphone, and a battery light if the candles aren't bright enough." She glanced about the church, where people were squeezing closer in pews to accommodate more comers. She giggled softly. "I hope none of those candles fall off their perches."

❧❧

DENNY CLOSED HIS BIBLE, stepped from the pulpit, walked to the front pew where Grace sat, and offered his arm. "You're on. Don't worry. You'll get up there, start reading, and forget all about being nervous. I have the diaries set up on the pulpit. Hannah had the section you're going to read typed out in large print to make it easier." He smiled at her. "And there's extra light, if you need it."

Grasping her sturdy cane and leaning on Denny's arm, Grace mounted the stairs separating the altar and pulpit from the congregation. She felt as if she were climbing a mountain. But the mountain flattened, and Denny led her to the pulpit.

"Will this do," he asked, "or would you rather sit?"

"I'll lean on the pulpit. I'm okay. I want to stand. Just hook up my mic."

That done, Grace turned to the papers on the pulpit. They would be a snap to read. The battery-operated lamp attached to the edge of the pulpit would be all the light she needed.

"Ladies and gentlemen," she began. "Amelia, Hannah, and I were blessed to come into possession of a very old tin box holding the diaries and letters of two men: John Foster, a Union soldier, and Tom Mueller, a Confederate soldier.

These men had been abandoned, left for dead in a ditch on a field after a battle.

"Miss Ella Mae Evans of this area had gone to this battlefield seeking her only grandson, and found him dead. She buried him there and while passing the ditch, she realized that the two men lying in it were alive. Miss Ella Mae gave them corn liquor to dull their pain, helped them to her old wagon, and brought them to safety. She cared for them and healed their wounds.

"You may ask, as we did originally, why Tom and John stayed with Miss Ella Mae after the war ended? They could have gone home. But she had tended them, and they had come to love her. She was old and alone in the high mountains, and there were also personal reasons. For John, a toss in the hay with a girl he didn't know or love resulted in a child and an unhappy marriage. Tom's mother had died when he was a boy and his father had remarried. There were many younger children at home, and Tom didn't care for his stepmother."

Grace's eyes scanned the audience. "Before you judge these men, remember they were mere boys at the time. Miss Ella Mae loved them, and they loved her and chose to stay with her. They settled down, farmed her land, raised cattle, and cared for her as if they were her sons until the day of her death."

There wasn't a sound, only expectant faces turned to her. Denny was right. Her fear had vanished. She had a story to tell, and a bit of Tom's and John's lives to share with these people gathered on this Christmas morning. She continued, sharing what they had learned about the men, about the women they had married, about the lives they had made for themselves in the mountains. Then Grace's tone grew lighter.

"So now, let me read to you the words of each man as he speaks about his past Christmases. I begin with John and Christmases in his hometown of Newtown, Connecticut." She slipped on her reading glasses.

> *When I was a boy, Christmas holidays began when we went to church on Christmas Eve. The minister didn't talk much, and I knew there'd be more singing than talking, which made me glad. I loved Annie Bale from school, and I could sit all day and listen when she was singing in the choir. Annie Bale had this voice you could hear above everyone, and she would be called on to come forward and sing by herself—sing to me, I thought.*
>
> *If you ask me what she sang or how the church was*

decorated, I couldn't say, but it must have been pretty. For all the way home, Ma kept talking about how nice the candles looked, and the greenery covering every post and beam and the railing of the upper floor.

Christmas morning, my sister woke me before the sun rose and we waited for Pa to say that Santa had come. Then we'd dash downstairs and scrabble to see who got the most presents under the tree.

I had put a present on Annie's desk the last day of school, when no one was in the room. Only I didn't say it was from me, and Jimmy Jakes said he'd given it to her. Annie started to like him and never looked my way again. It broke my eleven-year-old heart, and taught me a good lesson about other people taking credit for what you do. I saw it happen a lot in the war, but I'm not gonna write about war and Christmas on the same page.

Pa got me a horse of my own the next Christmas. It was stabled out at Uncle's farm. After dinner, we all got in the wagon and drove out there. I don't know when I have ever been so excited about any gift. All my cousins and my sisters and brother wanted to ride. Uncle put a saddle on Sky. That's what I named him, for the sky was so clear and blue, and seemed so close that day. We all had a ride, most of us with Uncle holding the *reins and walking us around his pasture. I learned to ride fast, and that summer I'd be out at Uncle's farm for days on end, until Pa got angry because I let so many of my home chores slip. Still, that was the best Christmas I ever had; the best present. Sky stayed with Uncle when I went off to war. War again—why must the war intrude into every good thing?*

Grace cleared her throat, shifted her weight, and sipped from a glass of water Denny had placed on a table nearby. How nice to have the attention of everyone focused on you. No wonder some ministers went on and on.

"Now I'll read from Tom's diary. Tom was not as well educated as John, but he was what I would call a deep thinker."

Christmas ag'in. We hauled us a right pretty tree to the house and decorated it with white stars cut out of paper Miss Ella Mae brung from her friend Miss Maggie. We set candles just like we done last year, and one of them stars caught fire. Miss Ella Mae doused it with a pot of water she'd set on the stove, and we quicklike took down all them white paper stars.

Made me think of a time at home in Walhalla, and

how Christmas Eve after church we'd go to Granny Gertie's house. Some folks we knew thought it weren't no good to celebrate Christ's birthday with trees and gifts and the like, or anyone else's birthday. I thought they was cheap and didn't want to spend no money on gifts for no one. I was sure glad Granny Gertie wasn't of that mind.

We'd sing together, all the family, even Uncle Kurt, who didn't much care if his brothers and sisters said he should keep his mouth full of food and not song. I liked Uncle Kurt. He'd give me a present every Christmas, and pat my head and say, "Ya, goot boy."

Grandpa talked about the snow back in the homeland, Germany. The old ones were forever talkin' 'bout the homeland. Mama once washed my mouth with soap fer sayin' they should go back there if they loved it so much.

Mama died the next Christmas. I was seven. Papa said big boys don't cry, so I cried out behind the woodshed where he couldn't hear me. Lord, I missed Mama. Papa stopped smilin' or laughin' or talkin' much. Our house went from bein' sunny to bein' stormy, and the storm never ended 'til I got here, and John and me brung Christmas cheer to Miss Ella Mae and to us, too.

Come Christmas, John and me got Miss Ella Mae a special present. We hired us a lady from the church to come to the house and sing songs that Miss Ella Mae's friend, Miss Maggie, said she had liked to sing, though I ain't never heard Miss Ella Mae sing no songs since I been here.

The lady sang "Curoo, Curoo" and Miss Ella Mae cried. John and me worried we'd done somethin' to hurt her, but she says no, she's cryin' fer joy. Then the lady sings "Once in Royal David's City" and "The Twelve Days of Christmas," which was the only one of them songs I ever heard. Miss Ella Mae hugged us right proper like we was her sons, and she says it was the best Christmas she ever done had. She's been like my mama ever since that day, and we make a big Christmas for her every year since that time.

Grace stopped. First there was silence; then they began to clap their hands. Clapping in church? Glancing over at Denny, she was amazed to see him standing and clapping. What should she do? Bow? Exit as fast as she could? Her eyes sought Bob's. Immediately he rose, and next thing she knew he was beside her assisting her back to the pew.

"Why did they clap like that?" she asked later as they waited for the church to clear.

"They were touched by the words you read, and by the caring and sincerity in your voice. And maybe, those who knew you knew about the accident, and were clapping to see you again."

"I was stunned. I didn't know what to do."

"You did just what you should do, nothing, and you left the pulpit and sat down and Denny finished the service with a few brief remarks." Bob looked around. "Good, the church is just about empty. We can go to the church hall without you being jostled or stopped a hundred times by well-wishers."

They started down the aisle. "I'm glad it's over," said Grace. "I couldn't sleep last night worrying about it, but once I started speaking and reading it was wonderful. People were so polite, quiet, and attentive."

"They were deeply touched by Tom's and John's stories—which, I might add, you told beautifully, with caring and empathy," Bob said.

WHEN SHE STEPPED INTO the church hall, Grace gasped. The ceiling was even lovelier then Amelia had described.

Glittering tiny lights resembled a star-filled sky. There were garlands of greenery everywhere and pots of lush, red poinsettias in the center of every table.

Family members milled about, finding one another and checking place cards on tables. Grace noticed a young woman switch her name from one table to another. Someone tapped Grace on the shoulder, and she turned to see Matthew Evans and a pretty woman.

"Grace, this is my wife, Maria. Maria, this is Grace." He looked at Grace. "We heard about your accident. Glad to see you up and about."

"What a terrible thing to go through," Maria said. "We are just so delighted to be here and to meet the Muellers and Penningtons from Walhalla. They said you came all the way down there to find them. They're such lovely people."

"I assume we'll all be getting copies of the letters and diaries?" Matthew asked. "We went to the house and read them. They touched us both very deeply."

"You can't read them without being touched," Grace replied. "Each family will have a set to take home with them. They'll be given out today. I hope you'll enjoy them as much as we have."

"It was most kind of you ladies, going to all this trouble, finding us, finding relatives we never knew we had,"

Matthew said. "I'll get down to Walhalla, finally, and get in some fishing. Arnold and Ada Pennington have a boat. They've invited us down to fish at Lake Jocassee."

"That's wonderful," Grace said.

"The letters gave us many hours of pleasure. We feel as if we know Thomas," Maria said.

Grace smiled, remembering the nights she lay in bed thinking about the men. "This gathering, bringing all of you together, was Amelia's idea."

"We must find her and thank her especially, then." Matthew's eyes searched the room, and moments later they were wending their way toward Amelia, who was standing by the buffet table talking to one of John's relatives from Newtown.

Grace looked about her. Happy to be alive, she moved about the room introducing herself to those she did not know, and welcoming others. After a time, standing strained her back, and she found a comfortable chair, sat, and enjoyed watching Amelia flit from table to table, from family group to family group. Amelia was so at ease with crowds of people. The years as hostess at her husband's Red Cross fundraisers had schooled her in the art of social pretense, she claimed, but Grace was certain that it was her innate charm and graciousness that set others at ease.

Hannah and Max bustled about a long table, where the green and red wrapped packages containing copies of the diaries and letters were stacked. Grace watched Max gather up an armful of packages and head toward the dining tables, then watched with a growing sense of excitement and pleasure as he set the Christmas gifts next to the poinsettia plants in the center of each table.

Then Milo, smiling ear to ear, stood at her side. With him were several women and a tall, portly gentleman. "Grace, I want you to meet my family from Newtown. This is my great uncle Henry and my cousins Lucille, Margaret, and Thea." His voice grew animated. "Uncle Henry's a professor of literature at the University of Connecticut in Hartford. Margaret heads the literature department at a community college, and Lucille and Thea teach at a Newtown high school."

"Quite a family of educators." Grace shook hands all around. The women were of the same height, neither tall nor short, and the resemblance to Milo was amazing. Thea differed from her sisters only in that she had long, dark, flowing hair and a smile that lit a room.

"Maybe it's in the genes," Margaret said.

They chatted for a time, then moved away to find their table, for the room had grown quieter as the guests found their tables and sat, and waiters moved about the room pouring champagne in fluted glasses.

At the head table Denny rose and lifted his glass, bringing silence. "Ladies and gentlemen, welcome to Covington. We are delighted that you made your journeys to be with us today, and we are honored by your presence. On each table sits a complete set of the writings of your kin. We hope you will enjoy and treasure them as we have. I am sure you'll be pleased to know that the original documents, the writings of John Foster and Tom Mueller, will be sent to the Library of Congress for preservation."

Everyone clapped.

Denny paused, the formal part of his comments over. "Amazing isn't it, and fortunate for us all that a tin box lay undisturbed in the earth for a century and a half, and that it came into the possession of three remarkable ladies who care about history, family, and *belonging*."

Grace felt a tingle run up her spine. *Yes,* she thought, *I belong here. My life is enriched by friends, love, and by this community of caring people. Could I ask for more? I'm a very lucky woman.*

". . . and our ladies and Milo Evans, whose genealogy skills facilitated the process, so that on this blessed Christmas Day we come together to share this holiday, this meal, and our lives." He paused and raised his arms to embrace all in the room. "On behalf of Grace, Amelia, Hannah, Milo, and all the folks who have made this evening possible, I welcome you. And I bless you all."

Then Denny lifted his glass. "A toast to your ancestors who left these records of their lives, and to the ladies and Milo for bringing us all together. A happy and a healthy Christmas."

Calls of "Hear, hear," and "Bravo" rose from all quarters of the room. Then the food was brought to each table: platters of turkey, bowls of stuffing, corn pudding, sweet potatoes, beans, and white mashed potatoes. While the families shared their meal, members of the church choir wandered the room in 1800s costumes, singing holiday carols.

It was five in the afternoon before the last guest departed, some tearfully, hugging one another and promising future visits.

It was six when the ladies and their men kicked off their shoes, put their feet up, and relaxed in front of the fireplace in Max's big living room. Max brought out the sherry and glasses and poured, then passed the tray and everyone took a glass.

"A toast to you ladies for your creative imaginations. You believed it was possible to find and reunite those families. You let no one discourage you. You took action, and your idea came to fruition."

"Let's drink to possibilities," Hannah suggested.

"And to hope," Amelia said.

"And to believing that your dreams can come true," Grace said.

"Merry Christmas to us all," Bob said. He looked at Grace and silently wished that she would be his wife.

And as the snow fell lightly outside, they sipped their sherry and smiled at one another. Soft wishes for a "Merry Christmas" mixed with the crackling of the fireplace, completing the warmth and good cheer that filled the room that Christmas night.